in the land
of the dinosaur

Also by Emily Meier

Suite Harmonic: A Civil War Novel of Rediscovery
Time Stamp: A Novel

Ten Stories and a Novella

in the land of the dinosaur

of the

EMILY MEIER

SKY SPINNER PRESS
SAINT PAUL, MINNESOTA

© 2011 by Sky Spinner Press
117 Mackubin Street
St. Paul, MN 55102
skyspinnerpress.com

Published in the United States of
America

Sky Spinner Press Books Distribution
through Itasca Books

itascabooks.com

ISBN 978-0-9836692-2-7

First Sky Spinner Press Printing, 2011

Library of Congress Catalog Control
Number: 2011911659

9 8 7 6 5 4 3 2 1

Cover and book design:
Jeenee Lee Design

Cover painting:
The Downs © Emily Ball

For Bob

CONTENTS

In the Land of the Dinosaur

On the wall of the Halley Bus Company, there is a map of the twisting route the school bus takes, picking up and returning the children of our area on its daily run. But the inner sense one has of this wide sweep of country is simpler than the map line. Make the bridge the starting point and the route is a plain loop which climbs and broadens toward the west and turns at the top, the loop pinching back on itself like a word bubble in a comic strip. It retreats from the house where Lawrence Lugar lives with his wife, Lawrence whose main wish in life has been that his son farm his land.

The whole stretch of countryside is as fine as one could find—a patch of old logged-out country, its plowed fields rimmed with a new growth of trees. In springtime, on the hills and bottomlands, a black-and-white spattering of dairy cows etches itself cleanly in the green world. There are no cows, though, at the beginning of the loop. Instead there is a hint of settlement, a dabble of houses beyond Klein's Bar with its sign for Wisconsin cheese, a tangle of roads and the aggressive rise of three hills, shaped like cabbages, that sidle back along the creek and shape the bends in the road where, when winter comes, cars can skid, losing the curve, and slide into the ditch, burying their hoods in snow. In winter, too, at four in the afternoon when the early drinkers at Klemper's Bar have seen the bus stop deep in the interior of the loop, the sun rolls down the curve of those hills and disappears.

Winter is our true season here. We have our summer days, of course, July days when all the air feels as boiled and heavy as the vapor in a summer kitchen. We have weeks at planting or harvest when clear skies and warm winds leave us dazed with utter pleasure. But shiver in a cold rain in August or glean corn in the dying fall, trudging along the sheared-off stubble of a backfield, and a sudden wind lodges winter in you as if it is the only season.

There is our winter sun, the pale circle that burns in a sky of lapis lazuli. There is the way the snow gusts across the valley in thin sheets and how all the children's swings in the yards along the creek road move riderless in the wind, how the heifers step through the ice of the creek on the bitterest days of cold to drink the water. And then there is Lawrence, who is retired from farming to a new workshop and an old pickup truck, and who lives with Pauline in a house next to the farm he sold when their son didn't want it. Lawrence still lives his life by the seasons.

"Have you got your wood in yet?" he asks his neighbors in April, pushing his cap so the brim shows the white of his forehead. Lawrence is a big man, a man whose body was never meant for ready-made clothing, and for work he dresses in overalls that hang limply to his ankles, his legs vaguely stick-shaped in outline and the fabric strained across his torso as if he were the filling and the overalls the cover of a giant stuffed bear.

"You got your wood in yet?" he asks again in June, still maneuvering around the year's central stretch of time—November to May—the way a ship in the Arctic skirts an iceberg. By the time he asks the question, his own wood is stacked long since, but there is still his chimney to be cleaned. After five years and as many arguments, he is used to it that Steve does it for him. On the first Saturday that feels like autumn, Lawrence waits next to the ladder and watches Steve climb to the roof where he clanks a metal expansion frame down the chimney, jerks it tight and hauls it back up, scraping the creosote away. Lawrence tills under the garden himself and mulches it with wet leaves. He walks the yard boundaries before the snow comes, a slow walk, his footsteps measuring the full three acres cut from the farm that used to be his and could have been Steve's, but isn't.

In the real winter of January afternoons, when Lawrence has stoked the fire in the living room stove, he stands at the dining room window and stares out at the fields. Sometimes—always if the arthritis in his hip is bothering him—he remembers the jarring earth under the tractor. He sees night. He is plowing and the tractor headlights pour an ivory mist like snow into the darkness. His eyes are tight with fatigue and he is lost for moments at a time on his own land until the feel of it comes back to him through the tractor seat.

But it is Jim Stone's land now, and Jim has started to talk about putting in trees. Lawrence cannot think about this without anger knotting his stomach, and if he mutters about neighbors turning socialist or stands too long at the window, Pauline, who on this January day leans back like clockwork from scraping potatoes at the kitchen sink to look out the front window for the school bus, will bring him some coffee, touch his shoulder.

The fields run like a spreading river west and north toward a ridge of hills. They are free of rocks in the light and in the distance. On the hills, trees rise against the sky and yet fall downward across the snow. Lawrence has explained this to his grandsons, how shadows are two different things: the one the sun's mirror when light streams between the trees, and the other the long, slanty twins of trees that flap down black on the snow from a hinge at their roots.

Trevor has grown too old to understand this. Or rather, Lawrence thinks, at twelve Trevor is suspicious, unsure that things are what they are said to be. Bennie, who is eight, can see that a hinge which is not metal or screwed in place or a thing you can feel, is a hinge nonetheless.

Silently, Lawrence tells himself again that Bennie is his favorite, that a man is allowed a favorite in his grandchildren, though it is not that he loves Bennie more. It is that Bennie, who stores his cars in the box under the window in Lawrence's workshop and draws streets on the floor in the sawdust, loves *him* more, that, most of all, Bennie believes everything Lawrence knows to be true, which is more than Lawrence feels about Trevor, and which is certainly more than he can say of Steve. Getting married in the other Lutheran church the way he and Joan did. Pauline still isn't over it and for that matter, Lawrence thinks, neither is he.

"Here it is now," Pauline tells him from the sink, and Lawrence walks out to the living room and watches the school bus slow down and turn right to go up the creek road. Pauline comes to look, pushing her glasses up on her nose, her fingers dimpled from the potato water. The taillights of the bus dip on the road and disappear around the curve.

After Sunday church, Lawrence drives up 12th Street to Steve's and heads up the walk carrying the anniversary cake Pauline has made. "You got their card?" he asks.

"In my purse."

"You put it in the collection plate."

"I did?" Pauline stops to fumble her purse open, and Lawrence laughs and nudges her toward the door.

Bennie lets them in and Lawrence hands him the cake. The house smells like beef stewing and like the crushed rose leaves and spices Joan stores in the gingham-covered bottles on her shelves. Lawrence pulls his overshoes off. He unwinds his muffler and takes his coat off and gives it to Pauline to put in the closet. He rubs his fingers. If he were at home, he'd head straight for the wood stove to warm up, but at Steve's house he counts on the dog or Bennie climbing on him so he can get thawed out.

Joan is on the phone in the kitchen doorway and she motions him to go on through. She holds the cord up for him. In the hallway to the family room, Lawrence thinks he hears the dog yowling outside, that she'll feel cold to the touch if he lets her in.

He stops at the window. There's a drift of snow at the end of the deck past the patio doors, but the rest of the deck is clear, and Lawrence stands admiring the forty-five-degree cut where the planks join at the corner of the kitchen and the family room. A good clean line from all the hours he spent measuring and getting the supports anchored right. The whole deck is as true now as it was three years ago when he put the last nail in. And ahead of schedule. They were still taping the walls in the family room. Joan hadn't finished her furniture stripping, let alone the upholstery, when this deck was ready for business.

Lawrence spots the dog collar and chain lying on the snow in the yard and wonders if Trevor's spaniel got loose, but then she bumps up against his ankles and reaches up pawing him.

"Get down, Ivy. Was that you woofing?" Lawrence pushes his knee into the soft fur of the dog's chest, and she moves backward into the family room, her tail wagging into Trevor, who's sprawled on the rug in front of the TV.

Bennie's on the couch. "Move over," Lawrence tells him. "You've got the whole thing to yourself. Where's your dad, Trevor?"

"Getting beer. Mom forgot."

"She can forget for me and Grandma both. How come the game's not on?"

"Watch Ivy, Grandpa. Come on, girl." Trevor rolls away from the TV and Ivy pushes her nose up to the screen and howls at a sumo wrestler. Trevor and Bennie are both giggling, and Lawrence pushes one of Joan's embroidered pillows behind his hip and untangles his pants leg. He laughs, too.

So it *was* Ivy he heard. "Turn the Packers on," he tells Trevor.

"They don't start until three."

"Then we'll watch the Vikings lose," Lawrence says, and Bennie, who could use a haircut, except that Joan likes his curls, squirms up next to him along with Ivy. "One of you smells like dog," Lawrence says.

In a while he hears Steve in the kitchen, and the refrigerator door opening and closing, and Joan talking before Steve comes out to the family room with a beer.

"Your damned dog chewed my glove, Trevor," Steve says.

"Wash up. Dinner's ready." Joan is in the doorway and Lawrence pushes on the couch arm to stand up.

"Turn up the TV," Steve tells Trevor, and Joan takes a sip of his beer and hands the can back. "Dad, you see what she did to her hair?"

Lawrence looks and realizes that that's what it is. Part of Joan's hair is lighter, streaked or something, when he'd thought she looked different just from having a dress on instead of jeans and a sweater. She still has her figure. Just like Steve is rock hard the way he was when he wrestled in high school, even if he ended up tall for a wrestler. Not that he ever got as tall as Lawrence. It got averaged out in Steve, Lawrence thinks, Lawrence's height and Pauline being short, though there isn't any average about his nose. With the hump in the middle, Steve's nose is nothing but Lugar.

Joan has her good dishes on the table. Pauline is pouring the milk for the boys when Lawrence sits down. It's a tight fit in the kitchen with all six of them at the table and Lawrence thinks, as he has been lately, that maybe he and Pauline can help with that, paying part for the dining room Joan wants added to face on the end of the deck.

Steve says the prayer and takes a scoop of potatoes. "God help us is right. Guess who came into Klein's with Richard Stosser," he says.

"I thought you were getting beer at the grocery store. You went all the way to Klein's?" Joan pours Steve's coffee and, hair streaks or not, Lawrence thinks how pretty she is. Her eyes are dark like Trevor's. They're quick like Bennie's.

"What about Richard Stosser?" Pauline's glasses are steamed over from the gravy and Lawrence thinks she looks like she's in the mountains somewhere, like a drift of cloud is caught on the bones under her eyes. Bennie bumps his milk over and Lawrence gives him his napkin to mop up.

He leans back in his chair. He's at Klein's in his head. That knock and roll of the pool ball. The sunlight warming the wood of the bar beside his Coke glass. *"Vous rêvez,"* the lady from Canada who worked there a season said to him once. She circled her hand in the air and then translated while he watched the sparrows on the roof of Klein's shed and the big hawk sailing along above the creek. "You dream," she told him.

Steve is talking, chewing his meat, telling how Art Klein was out back getting ice and how Richard came walking into Klein's with Cheryl Kay wrapped around him. Judy's sister.

Judy Kay. Judy Kay, Richard Stosser's wife who had the colt she was raising from foal that waited all snowy-faced for her to lean over the fence post with a sugar cube—Judy Stosser who called Richard at Klein's, screaming on the phone for him to come home, and when he walked in, pulled the trigger on a pistol in her face.

"The girl must be touched," Pauline says.

"If she's with Richard, she gets touched for sure," Steve says. He wipes his mouth with his napkin.

Joan, Lawrence realizes all at once, isn't saying a thing.

She's still quiet after the cake. Except for the thank-you, she's even quiet when she opens the card with the two checks Pauline wrote out, one for her, one for Steve. Thirteen dollars each, a dollar apiece for every year they've been married.

"So you can buy your own dinner if I take you out Tuesday," Steve says, and Joan gets up, clearing the table.

Lawrence heads out to the living room and the window chair.

When the sun shines in low and wakes him up, he can still hear the TV. He sees Pauline bundled up out front watching Bennie build a fort while Ivy dives in the snow. Lawrence takes his handkerchief out to blow his nose. He gets up to go to the bathroom, and he hears Steve and Joan talking in their bedroom. He waits by the hallway, wondering if he should cough a couple of times and then go ahead and walk past their door. He tinkers with his hearing aid.

But he can't tune out Steve's voice. "You got any more accusations? It's your idea to split up and you can goddamn well be the one that tells them."

Lawrence's heels settle against the floor. He fumbles his handkerchief into his pocket and feels the sharpness, the pressure in his bladder. He backs up, knocking into a table. He moves away from his shadow on the floor, away from the hanging quiet in the bedroom.

They can stop at a gas station. He and Pauline can stop so he can use the restroom, he thinks, and he gets the closet open and takes his coat out.

"Dad?"

"We're going now." Lawrence remembers his muffler on the shelf but he leaves it there and pulls his coat on, heading toward the door, fumbling, reaching for the knob to let him out.

In February, long after the flight of herons and eagles, of geese honking south, the snow is iced with a blue sheen. On Saturdays, Lawrence and Bennie search for abandoned corn pickers. Dinosaurs. They find them blackened with rust, derelict in fields, their long chutes angled and bent over in heads.

Bennie spots a sixth and a seventh one in the northwest corner of the county, their metal faces rearing up behind the treetops near the river bottoms. Braking, Lawrence pulls the truck over and lets the engine idle, and Bennie undoes his seatbelt and kneels up to lean against the windshield so he can see better.

"They're frozen into the snow," Lawrence says. "Just like houses and trees. In the winter, everything gets stuck."

"Houses can't move, Grandpa."

"They can when a twister hits. And they can settle. You're not going to tell me a tree can't move?"

"It's people that move." Bennie sits back down and the seat springs bounce.

"Want a closer look?"

Bennie shakes his head. He pushes at the glove compartment

with his foot, trying to open the latch, trying to get scolded, Lawrence thinks.

Lawrence shifts the truck into gear and pulls back onto the highway. "Seven. There's a lucky number," he says.

But even he's not buying what he's said. Luck schmuck. It's all left, he thinks—gone south with the birds after all the trouble they've had. Steve in a two-room apartment in town. Moved out. Trevor and Bennie staying over with Pauline and him on Fridays so Joan has a night free, and Trevor sleeping till noon just like a teenager. And now Bennie getting pouty and literal-minded.

He's been over it and over it with Pauline. At three in the morning, when she asks if he's awake and he is, they talk about it. Sometimes she puts her glasses on and gets up and goes to the bathroom in her slippers to get the pills the doctor prescribed. If Lawrence has the sheets churned up, she pulls at them, tucks them flat, talking about the boys, about bruised apples going bad. She tours the bedside. She tells him again how she's said to Joan it takes waiting some, that she knows Steve's a handful, that she raised him, didn't she? She tells Lawrence the whole thing's like a disease that came in on the road from town, and he tells her no, that Steve and Joan are in town, that whatever it is, it didn't need to travel.

"They aren't real dinosaurs anyway," Bennie says, his foot still pushing on the latch, and Lawrence looks over at him and turns off the highway onto the creek road.

When they get home, Trevor is in his pajamas eating toast and eggs. Lawrence tells him to finish up, to get dressed and fill the wood bin before his mother comes, and then he checks the stove and cuts a piece of bread for himself and goes on out to his workshop. He fidgets his tools into order. In a while he hears Joan's car in the driveway and he gets busy sweeping. He feels the sun on the broom handle, and Bennie comes in wearing his jacket and boots.

Lawrence sits down on his workbench, holding the broom. He touches the spot next to him, but Bennie stays standing, ready to go.

"I'm supposed to hurry. Grandpa, maybe they *used* to be dinosaurs."

Lawrence shakes his head. "They're dinosaurs now," he says. "Think about it. They look like dinosaurs, and they've got no earthly purpose left. That's a dinosaur, Bennie."

When Bennie has gone, Lawrence hears a car start and pull away. He puts the broom back in the corner. He can count to ten, and Pauline will be at the door asking, since he didn't come out, if he's as mad at Joan now as he is at Steve for whatever it is Steve did or didn't do, if he's mad at Joan for her part in the whole thing or maybe for something else. But it goes past being mad, he thinks. It goes to something he doesn't even have a name for.

He hears Pauline's footsteps, and he starts sanding a wooden flower for her window box.

"Lawrence?"

He's got his answer ready. He didn't feel like seeing Joan, is all. And what is there to talk about anyway when it's turned out like this after all the things he and Pauline did to help out? With the house and all. With the boys.

Lawrence looks over his shoulder, waiting, and he thinks Pauline is right about her hair. They did get the curls too tight at the beauty parlor. Her whole scalp is like it's jacked up a notch.

She sits down on the workbench. She picks at her apron. "Joan said she's having the divorce papers served on Monday."

Lawrence feels the knock in his stomach. For a moment he just stands there, he just looks at the shelves, and then he takes a slow turn around the workbench. He taps the flower on his knuckle, so the sawdust falls off. He puts the sandpaper down. Finally he looks at Pauline. "It's come to that," he says.

She nods. She winds an apron tie around her hand. "Lawrence, those kids aren't getting back together. That's what it's come to."

In our countryside, in the long loop the school bus takes, there is always idle talk, gossip at times, at times something more. You can hear about the farm that spreads on both sides of the main county road and hosts an endless race between the multiplying number of dogs and children and the abandoned farm machines. You can talk about the couple that moved away and returned in a single year, their taste for adventure trimmed to raising llamas instead of cows. And there is always a list of facts to discuss: why it is people drive down the middle of the road and some of them drive *fast* down the middle of the road; how a fondness for VCRs and snowmobiles never counts much next to the sounds of cattle lowing in spring when the calves are born, of kids jumping in the creek in summer; how parties always mean Jell-O salads and white buns and a wedding means spoons clinking in a church basement for the bride and groom to kiss and, if the wedding day is hot, somebody like Steve Lugar saying he sure hopes the groom's got himself an air-conditioned room for the night.

There aren't that many secrets in the country. There's a kind of rural therapy that says you tell the hard with the good, and so Pauline is on the phone all afternoon with her sister and with her nieces, and Lawrence, who's helping the new neighbors load up their pickup with some of his extra wood, is talking, too.

"Steve's got his apartment since Joan kicked him out. Now they're getting divorced," he says.

At night, though, all the words are gone and Lawrence snores himself through unspeakable dreams. He moans. He turns, murmurs, driving a face away—Joan's face, though it's tightened with Pauline's curls and split by a snake's tongue that catches and probes through a dark snag of velvet. The tongue swells purple, explodes in a skyburst of seed.

Pauline is talking at three in the morning: "Are you here or asleep?"

"Tell her to go home. Tell Joan to leave," Lawrence says, and he startles awake.

"So they've got you talking in your sleep." Pauline straight-arms her pillow, shifts it around, and she starts on a new recital of events, second guessings.

Lawrence nods into his own pillow, but he doesn't answer. He feels heavy, his mind still thick with a coating of dream.

Slowly the room catches up. The alarm clock glowing from the dresser. The ridges of his thumbnail against his forehead. Pauline's voice is a bumblebee's hum.

But the dream lingers. Once he might have burned with such a thing, faulted himself. Now though, with the pendulum cadence of Pauline's talk and the plain faithfulness of a long life, his conscience is free. He loves Joan. He likes her prettiness, her hard work. She's been a daughter, and if his mind has wandered into Steve's in the night, he's had a dream and that's all it is.

He's explained such things to the boys—that thoughts untangle in sleep but they start wrong sometimes. They get like a yo-yo string, twisted up more before they unwind. It's a thing to grow used to, accept.

Yet even so, he does not sleep well again until the sermon at church. This time Pauline wakes him with a hand on his elbow. The church rustles with people. It is warm with their heat, with light glowing through stained glass.

Our church, Lawrence thinks. *Our church.*

He feels its years enclosing him. His parents' funerals. His marriage to Pauline. Then Steve's baptism, Pauline fussing to keep the gown free of wrinkles—to keep it just as her mother had done, the history of their care pristine in impeccable folds. It was his part to worry instead about a boy in a dress and to fear that the pastor, grown old and palsied, would drop Steve, would lose his footing and dash the soft spot of Steve's head against the baptismal font. He stayed poised for a catch, frowning until the water was poured, until Steve cried and Pauline opened her breast to him in the darkness of the back hall.

They had known already that Steve was an only child, that the hemorrhage that followed his birth was a rupture of something important. But a *son*. Lawrence stood guard. Pauline was still pale. Her face was as absent of color as the white breast Steve pushed up and down against her coat.

Yet Steve did not marry in this church.

Steve does not farm.

Steve is getting divorced.

Lawrence opens the hymnal, his fingers catching on its pages. He hunts for the pitch, and Pauline is singing beside him, her voice lowered, burred with the years.

On the last Monday of February, blizzard warnings are out for the whole county. Lawrence works through the morning bringing in wood, chipping ice off the downspout and then renailing its supports which blew loose in the last wind. He wraps the tape higher on the apple trees so the rabbits, if they get a taller perch from a new snow, won't strip the bark. When he goes inside, it's past one. Pauline tells him he's working too hard and he tells her he's not, raising his voice, surprising them both.

She stands with her back to the sink. She looks at him and, with all the things she's told him in the last weeks, the things she won't say are clearer on her face. Or clear to him. She's confused at how he's taken Joan's part more than Steve's and then acted distant with Joan; she's sure that he wants so much from Steve, and always has, that he handles it by asking too little. But she will not say this out loud. He knows that she won't. If she did, he'd answer she was the one who spoiled Steve, and they would both have done it then: accused each other of the blame for their whole family breaking apart.

"I thought you'd have dinner ready," Lawrence says, his voice quieter, and Pauline takes his plate from the microwave and puts it on the table. He sees her plate standing in the dish drainer, and he realizes he had his hearing aid off, that he wouldn't have heard her when she called.

She gets him a glass of milk and sits down. She puts her elbows on the table. "Steve phoned. Joan had the papers served."

Lawrence looks up from a meatball. "At work?"

"On his break." Pauline drums her elbows with her fingers. Then her shoulders start to shake and she pulls her apron up to her face, and she's sobbing into the cloth, her glasses all cockeyed on her forehead.

Lawrence gets up awkwardly and stands by her chair. He remembers what Pauline's sister said—that Steve is good to the kids and brings home a big check, that maybe on the inside Joan's like the pickles that get flat sour, that maybe when they did her hair, they bleached something out of her head.

Lawrence considers all this and thinks it's unfair. For all that that girl came out of—the poorness of the family, neglect even—and how it's like a rule with her to make things nice, to work hard. The boys all spit-polished for big occasions and, at least once before, her forgiving Steve. But it's different this time, something deep down between the two of them that Steve probably did without even thinking how it would make her feel small, how it would drop the heart right out of her.

Yet still, it might be impatience. Like Pauline says, the whole thing could be about Joan not waiting long enough. And if it's that, who knows? She could sell the house, and there'd be another family on his deck. Joan could move to Texas like her girlfriend did and take the boys. It could mean anything, Lawrence thinks. Anything at all.

"I'm done blubbering." Pauline says, wiping her eyes with the apron. Her voice is full of hiccoughs, and Lawrence goes to the sink to get her some water.

She's still shaky. "At least it's better than Stossers. I'd rather they were divorced than shot."

"That was different. Mental," Lawrence tells her, and saying it, he's sure that it's true.

But he feels out of sorts. His bowels are unsettled. In his workshop, he tries carving the dinosaur he's making for Bennie, but the head isn't right. He looks at Pauline's flowers. Then he just sits.

The storm won't come. The clouds hang. They're so gray that they're almost brown; they're so heavy that Lawrence thinks the snow, when it finally does arrive, will just drop, will cover everything in one, great, massive clog.

Pauline comes in and stands at the window and says what she's said before, that it's like a baby that's due and won't start.

By suppertime, the forecast has changed. Lawrence stares at the TV and talks to himself: *So what if they say the real storm has moved north? There's no sky with these clouds. There're no stars.*

It's a grayness that lasts all week, a grayness that seems to settle inside him. Even on his card night Lawrence feels gloomy, even on Wednesday when he takes Pauline for groceries and they stop at the Moose lodge. Steve doesn't come for supper. Trevor calls about his shop project, and Bennie gets on the extension to say Ivy can walk backward on her hind legs. Lawrence wants Friday to come. He wants the boys actually to *be* here so he can show Trevor how to do a bevel, so Bennie can crawl in with them if he has a nightmare that won't go away.

Pauline tells him he doesn't have to wait, that the boys can come over early or he can go to their house like always, that of course Joan will let him in.

Lawrence shakes his head. Maybe he's stubborn, but it's like a schedule now. *Friday.* Friday even when the week seems stuck, when it's like Tuesday went twice or Thursday got doled an extra shift.

When Friday actually comes, Lawrence wakes up and the weather has changed. Outside, emptying the ash bucket and filling the bird feeders, he thinks the air has a moistness in it like spring. He puts the birdseed back in the garage and goes into the kitchen to get breakfast. Pauline has his eggs ready. She's made juice with the squeezer.

"I'm hanging the rugs out," she says. Lawrence nods and figures she's thinking spring like he is, though they both know it's a whole lot too early.

"We do have a blue sky," he says. "A skimpy blue, but it's blue."

He stands up from the table and, when he turns the damper down on the stove in the living room and goes into his workshop, he can tell she's been there before him. Everything's swept and there's dust in the air. She'll be cooking, too, he thinks, making the caramel cake that Bennie likes.

By noon he's sanded the last triangle on the dinosaur's back and he's stirring up paint. He has cans set on the shelf—a pea green that will dry down, black, and a darker green, and then the leftover red from Trevor's fire engine. He turns the radio on for the farm report and goes straight out to find Pauline. "Can you believe that?" he asks. "Now it's cleared up, they say it'll snow."

At two o'clock, when he's wishing he'd started earlier on the paint so it would be dry enough to put the scale marks over the green, the sky has clouded up and the first flurries start. Pauline's rugs are flecked with white on the clothesline. She's on the path Lawrence has cleared all winter, taking them down, shaking the snow off.

He opens the kitchen door to let her inside. "I told you," he says. "How come you made ginger cookies? It smells like Joan's. They'll think they're at their house."

In the living room, he puts more wood in the stove. Pauline points at the window. "We've got visitors," she says.

Lawrence pushes his back straight, standing up. Jim Stone's heifers are in the yard. Lawrence reaches for the telephone and dials. He lets it ring, but nobody answers.

"Is that one going for the rosebush?" Lawrence puts the phone down and gets the door open yelling *Shoo!* and waving his arms while the cows stare at him and then trot off toward the fields and turn back to stare more.

Lawrence hunts for tracks out the back window. He can't see any, but cows are cows. If they've got spring fever early, it's still likely they got out the same old way—by the back hill where the fence broke before.

"Keep shooing. I'll find the break," he tells Pauline.

"Don't go out. It's snowing harder."

"It's not snowing hard."

Lawrence puts his jacket on. He has his muffler wrapped around his neck and his hat on with the flaps down. His big boots are in the garage, and he gets them and pulls them on and finds his padded gloves and fencing tool and a roll of barbed wire and a bag of metal clips. He takes his sledgehammer down in case the fence posts are out, in case they're pushed up with the frost. But it figures, he thinks. You sell your farm to somebody and then you've got his cows in your yard.

Pauline is in the kitchen doorway. Lawrence knows she has him on the casualty list for the three hundredth time: the man who died two feet from his own back door in a whiteout. He tells her again to keep shooing and he asks her to clean his brushes, too, to make sure the paint lids are tight. "And try Jim Stone again. Tell him we're having that star-face for supper."

"Lawrence," she says.

In the shed, he uncovers the snowmobile. He checks the oil, and then the gas and runners. He knows if it takes very long, Trevor and Bennie will be here when he gets back, so he puts on a helmet for the example, though it makes him feel foolish. The Green Bay Farmer, but here he goes.

He follows the fence. It climbs the hill to the north of the creek. The wind burns his face and when the runners dip with the earth, he rides back high into the sting of the snow. He was right about what he told Pauline. It's not snowing hard. It's a quiet snow, a small snow, but it bites from the wind and the speed that he's going. He leans left, steering along the fence, angling upward toward the trees. He throttles down, easing over the crest of the hill and coasting right at the "T" where the fences cross. He stops. He lets the motor idle. It's like a buzz saw, and he switches it off.

Silence. The wind muffled in the trees, the snow like the afterthought of hay that follows bales down when they're thrown from a loft.

But so white. So incredibly white.

Lawrence takes the helmet off and puts the roll of wire over his shoulder. He can walk from here. The snow is drifted, but it's packed, crusted on top, and when he does break through, it's not really deep. He sinks in only to boot-top. He can make his way. He can move along the fence, eyeing whole valleys of snowed-in fields and his own back yard. Both his back yards. The one with Pauline's clothesline in it and the one with the upended birdbath that belongs to Grace Stone. There's a plume of smoke from the chimneys on both places, and there's frost on the wood of the barn. His barn. The cow barn. Well, Jim's barn.

Lawrence closes his eyes against the snowflakes. For a second he can see what might have been. The path worn over the hill from Bennie and Trevor coming to visit. The place all spiffied up Joan's way. A white fence even. No birdbath but Joan's trellises by the back porch where Pauline had her roses. Steve with a new tractor ready to plow in the spring, Steve laying down the straightest furrows in the county.

The thought is so strong that it's almost a memory. It catches Lawrence, grips him until his foot bites down through the snow again, and he reaches to steady himself against a post.

But Steve wanted a paycheck, the weekends off. And it wasn't Joan. It was that the land didn't hold him; it was the land Steve never could see.

Lawrence uncoils the wire. He's spotted the break: two snapped wires over churned up snow, and then a half-covered trail which starts off north and turns east.

He could use a tractor, but not with this snow. For a second he thinks of the snowmobile, of using it to lead the wire and pull it tight. But the motor could stall. It could overheat which is too big a problem for a favor done from necessity, from annoyance really, though what was Jim thinking anyway?—a three-wire fence in a place where his cows have been out. A heavy snow—one that weighed down the lowest wire—and the cows could stroll right through, leave without breaking a thing.

Lawrence twists the wire ends and hooks the clips on the posts. There is sweat in the small of his back. He pulls the fencing tool from his pocket and squeezes the clips ends closed and runs another two wires below the first one, and all the time the snow is falling like the last fine puff of flour from a sifter.

He pushes his cap back. He sticks his tongue out, touching cold and the sky. This airy, snow softness. The sinking sun pale in the clouds. The old snow powdered matte and the new snow so thin he can see for miles—roads, six farms, six silos, the township schoolhouse unused except for 4-H. In the farthest distance, curved fields stack up. They're pancaked straight like the cross sections of rock in Trevor's earth science book.

Lawrence blinks them back flat. He checks the fence again, pulling the wire. He stuffs the fencing tool in his pocket and hangs the last of the barbed coil of wire on his shoulder and turns around.

To the east, on the far side of the creek, the school bus is nosing over the hill. It comes down the road. It stops by Stones' place, its red lights doing the hula, and Lawrence thinks he can call the Stone kids to herd the cows in, though Jim will be back. Before long Jim will be milking.

Lawrence watches through a scrim of snow. The bus rolls north. It slows to a stop, this time for Friday. The lights go on and he sees Trevor and then Bennie behind him, smaller on the road. A long scroll of color is blowing from Bennie's knapsack and it sails free, a winter kite, a red-mouthed green dinosaur alive in the wind. Bennie reaches for it, running toward the creek road and, from the east, a car careens around the curve rushing westward over the snow. Down the middle of the road, *fast* down the middle of the road.

Lawrence is running, crashing through the snow, yelling for someone to know what he sees, the gossamer, the horrible danger of this flying car, and Bennie its target.

And in freeze frame then, it is over. The cows have meandered into the road and the car has rocketed past and swerved left, missing them, missing Bennie by only an inch, and Lawrence was not there. Like a creature with no earthly purpose, he was simply not there.

Lawrence touches his neck, reaching to feel of the dryness, the outer case of his throat. The house blocks his view, but he knows that the boys have gone inside, that Pauline is hugging and scolding, that her heart beats fast through her hugs. Already the school bus is far up the creek road. The cattle are shredding the paper dinosaur, churning it into the road, scarring the tracks of the car.

And Bennie is safe, an idea so palpable it is like crystal, a physical lightness and weight.

Lawrence stands on the hill. Along the creek road and past Stones', snow haloes lights: lights in windows, on barns, on a solitary pole. Like ringed points on a map they stop space. In the snowy twilight, the road to town ends in the darkness before Klein's Bar.

The Home of the Wet T-Shirt Contest

It was never a secret June Klemper was obsessed. Long before Klemper's Bar was Reed and Vera's instead of Reed and June's, she was dying to make it as successful as Klein's—as solid and just as much the favorite place to stop in the southeast part of the county. At one time or another, all the Klemper's regulars had talked about it, including Otto Baakey, who was Klemper's best customer and June's biggest fan. Even her mother, visiting from Arizona where she'd retired and then gone into real estate, had launched into the subject when June drove her back to the airport.

"If you wanted number one, you should've married Art Klein instead of Reed Klemper," she said. "Honey, it's location first, second, and third. You can make it work for you that Klemper's is the out-of-the-way place to go, but don't expect the traffic Sue and Art get."

June listened and she didn't listen. She studied the bar, deciding if curtains on the windows over the pool table would be cheery or too domestic. She tried yellow ones and took them down. She tried them tie-dyed until Tarr Hansen asked if she'd been to Woodstock. She thought hard about a new beer sign for the pole, wondering whether a Leinie's or Bud fluorescent would be more visible from far away and which one would have the most eye appeal. And every month when she figured out the bar income and it was below what she'd been hoping for, she was grouchy and yelled at the kids until Reed started calling her mood that time of the month.

The really critical phase, though, started the day in 1980 when she drove past Klein's Bar on the way to town and saw the lot full and a great big cab tractor sitting halfway into the road and cars parked clear past the roller rink. It didn't calm her down a bit to hear from Knobby Hansen that Klein's had simply caught the overflow from the new aerobics class that had half the polyester pants in the county going st-retch in the roller rink and the teacher yelling "touch your knees, girls," and everybody panting in and out. June, who thought Klemper's had the prettiest spot in the whole creek valley, was beside herself with jealousy.

"All Klein's has is weed trees," she said to Reed when she got back. "The sumac and maple's on fire here. We got new asphalt, and they're the ones with the cars parked all over each other to find a place. What's it going to be like in deer season?"

Reed didn't answer. He wiped his cloth over the bar and opened up another can of Tab for Otto, who was getting ready to play pool and was retired from writing for the newspaper and from drinking, too.

"We should have a promotion," June said. "Otto, tell Reed we should. It's eight weeks to deer season and last year Klein's had all the out-of-state business. You ever hear of running a business without promoting it? They even had people from Chicago."

"I never heard of a pool table that kept the balls when you put your money in."

"Hit the side," June said. She took her coat off and got the money slot unjammed.

For days, then, she thought about the possibilities. She wanted something besides a deer hunter's special, though she was considering that, too, and mixing drinks Tarr Hansen kept trying even when Otto told him getting drunk on beer and peppermint schnapps wouldn't do a thing for his reputation as a serious drinker. She was thinking maybe some kind of exhibit—Civil War muskets or Indian hunting knives, though Reed shook his head when she mentioned it.

"Where're you going to find all that?" he said, popping a Tab for Otto. "Listen to her. She's planning to arm the customers if they don't bring their own. Yesterday she was talking polka bands. The deer hunters I know are trying to get away from women. You ever hear anybody that went hunting so he could polka with them?"

"I'd polka with this girl," Otto said, patting June's wrist, and she stopped mixing her newest concoction and leaned over the bar and kissed him.

"You're an idea man, Otto," she said smiling her best dark-eyed smile. "What do you think we should do?"

"Maybe a pony pull like Klein's had. I don't know, June. Something about the public's right to know, I'd have a notion. But this isn't that and I don't."

June got busy washing the bar glasses because Otto, with his fleshy face and bad heart and his memory for the name of everybody in the whole county and half the dogs, had just reminded her of her dad before he died. But she still wanted an idea. She was still determined. And she thought maybe Reed was softening a little. He'd rolled up his sleeves so the twin eagles showed and he dried the glasses for her and said if she'd get a sitter he'd have his nephew tend bar on Friday so they could go to a movie.

"Maybe I'll put out a suggestion box," June said.

"Here's something for you, Reed." The bar was mostly empty, but Tarr Hansen was still sitting way down at the last stool by the cooler the same as he always did. He pointed at his newspaper, the smoke from his cigarette curling over his head. "June, you want Reed to get rich, you can have yourself a wet T-shirt contest."

June put the glass she was washing back in the sink. "T-shirts? Maybe. We could give out shirts with the Klemper's name in big letters and maybe a logo. Something with a deer. What do you mean wet?"

Reed had gone down to the end of the bar, and he was looking at the newspaper. He turned the page to the inside and kept on reading. Then he set the paper down. "You got your promotion right here, June," he said grinning. "Read all about it."

He handed her the paper and June started reading and then stopped, looking at Reed. "Reed Klemper, what are you talking about? This bar's a family establishment."

"There aren't any families when it's deer season," Reed said. "Anyway, everybody here goes north."

"Who do you think you'd get to do it, the Homemakers' Club? You said they were trying to get away from women." June was scowling, and she dumped Tarr's ashtray out and set it down where he couldn't reach it.

"I'll get us some college girls," Reed said, and Otto racked up the balls, and Tarr stood up to get the ashtray. He was laughing.

"You got the idea, Reed," he said lighting another cigarette. "Those college girls'll do anything."

"Not in my bar they won't," June said, lifting Tarr's pizza out of the microwave.

"I guess they will," Reed said.

"You can get serious, Reed Klemper."

"I am."

"Over my dead body."

For days, then, it was a wrangle, June saying they were in Wisconsin not California, and Reed, who everybody knows has as little temper as a man can have but who can turn absolutely stubborn when his back is up, saying if she wanted the money she had her chance, and the customers who came into the bar adding their two cents' worth until June realized one day that business had already picked up.

"A wet T-shirt contest or nothing?" she asked Reed.

"You got that right."

"I don't suppose there'd be much of anybody we know. I can't see Klein's getting all the trade."

"You be here, Otto?" Reed asked.

"If I had the heartbeat for a thing like that anymore. No," Otto said, pushing his eight ball into the pocket, but Reed kept waiting and finally Otto said OK.

They scheduled the contest for the Friday in deer hunting week, and when it was set, June asked her sister if she'd take the kids since she figured the less Reed's mom knew about what was going on, the better. Reed had his nephew Charlie line the girls up and put up posters at the college and bring in an amplifier June thought just might shake the paneling off the nails. She wrote the ads for the county newspaper herself after Otto told her what she should say, how she should emphasize the up-to-date aspect of the contest and the scholarship money for the winner. She put up signs in the bar, too, and went out of her way to make them tasteful.

There were people who told her she was wasting her money to advertise at all since word about a thing like that travels fast, and everybody in the county knew what was up even before whoever it was took red paint and wrote "Home of the Wet T-Shirt Contest" under the Klemper's Bar sign one night. Otto told her the contest was a topic all over the place, including a few pulpits, and there'd even been talk of forming a delegation to ask Reed to call the whole thing off. At the bar, when the subject came up it was more by indirection, men who hadn't missed looking for deer up north in thirty years saying that, due to the energy crisis, they were thinking of staying close to home, and women who'd complained for years about hunting season, saying their husbands were going north if they had to drive them themselves. June had a bad night or two, waking up with her old choked-off dreams about her dad catching her with Reed in the pickup truck when she was still in school—and Reed said once he wished she'd just settle for what they had, but mostly they were businesslike about it, and June spent her free time working on charts for putting in extra tables where they wouldn't violate the fire code. With one ear she listened to Otto carry on about the girl who lived past the creek road and was still hanging out laundry, even in the snow.

"All that pink and blue wash freezing by the evergreens. If she washes for her congregation for a penance, what's it a penance for? What kind of outfit has a penance like that?"

June chewed on her pencil and looked at the table in the corner.

"I don't know, Otto. Maybe it's for keeping her kids like they're scrubbed and starched to death." June got up and poured a beer for Arnold Tilson, who'd come in from digging his last grave of the season and was already so far into celebrating that he was talking about drilling for oil in his front yard.

When she sat back down, Otto had switched to talking about Julie Hanover, Jed's wife. "How come she'd walk out on a thing like that?" he said. "Think about it. So OK, she's a ban the bomber. And so she got in thick with that pastor who chained himself to the courthouse. But how come a grown woman's moved to England to protest about missiles at some air force base when she's got a family to raise right here in this county? You know anybody else that owns a good business and had a tryout with the Brewers like Jed did?"

"Did you take your medicine, Otto?" June said, touching his sleeve and wondering how many other people made their money listening to people think out loud.

On the night of the contest, June drove the kids to her sister's. When she got there, she thought she'd just like to stay. Josie had a pot of chili on and the baby was bubbly, a happy little chunk, and the older kids had their board games out. Josie took her kids' coats. "Don't worry about them," she said. "I hope you and Reed don't get arrested."

Driving back, June was nervous, rattled. In the afternoon she and Reed had closed the bar to get things set up and she'd been so hyper that finally Reed just picked her up and carried her back to the shower. He'd sudsed her up, sang in her ear, tapped the "Star-Spangled Banner" on her back and loved her and loved her until she cried from relief, holding on to the wet hair on his chest. Now, though, she was wound up again, tight as a drum.

The headlights and moon dimly lit the creek road as she drove. It was quiet, a place like church where you sometimes found a silence that had a shape. She slowed the car to a stop and unrolled the window. She listened. Then she felt something as much as she heard it, a slow, dim rumble that came through the earth. Thunder? An earthquake? She sat a moment longer. Then, with a growing apprehension, she rolled up the window and went on.

When she turned onto the T of their own road, she was in a traffic jam. It was still a half a mile to the bar, but the road was all parked up and there were trucks backing up to find a place and lights in her rearview mirror. The noise was louder now. She could hear it with the windows up.

She pulled at her coat sleeve and looked at her watch. Six o'clock. Two hours until the contest started and it was bedlam already and, with Charlie working on the sound system, Reed would be tending bar by himself. She felt panicked. She drove down the road looking for a place to park. Then she took a chance and went straight on, hoping there was wiggle space left in the driveway to get the car up to the garage, but when she found a spot big enough for her Pinto between two pickups, she squeezed it in. She quick-checked her lipstick in the mirror and pushed her bangs back to the side and thought that for a moderately cute small person with three kids but a good, tight body, she looked OK. She got out of the car and started up the road, her sneakers crunching on the snow, and she walked fast, not stopping to talk to anybody. Hardly anyone was a stranger, which surprised her, but she felt scared anyway. The road was already full of beer cans. Men were laughing and shouting at each other, walking and flipping snowballs, and she could hear the pounding bass from the sound system in the bar and some kind of screaming on top that got louder with every step she took. She was the only woman around and, in a sea of orange jackets, she knew she was the only idiot in a deer's brown coat.

When she was closer to the bar, she saw Otto. He was coming down the road from his house and he saw her, too, and waited.

"It sure smells like beer, like maybe it rained beer," he said. He fell in beside her, walking. "Lord, June. I heard this racket before I was out my door. What've you got in there? Reed have an animal in a leghold trap? I heard that kind of music that crawls up your entrails after the war, but I never thought I'd hear it on American soil."

Otto kicked the snow off his boot and looked around. "You got hunters who said they were going north coming in from the opposite direction they usually do. I'd say you've got the whole county here."

"We've had it full before," June said. She was thinking of the party Grace and Rollie Vonns threw for their twenty-fifth anniversary and the night the bowling team won the league. But when Otto opened the door and they went inside she knew she needed another word besides full. There were people everywhere. There were so many at the bar it looked like just one long line of glasses from end to end, and there were people sitting three to a chair and on the pool table and the shuffleboard. It was mostly men, but the women and girls who were there were on somebody's lap and there was so much smoke in the air it looked like the streaks of fog in the morning hills. It was just crammed, crammed the whole way to the wall with people, and the air that was left was nothing but noise, all the screaming music and people talking so their voices went together in one ear-breaking, gigantic buzz. June squeezed her way up to the bar. She started pouring beer. She glanced at Reed, but he was fixing drinks and his eyes were working the whole room as if he were keeping it together that way, hemming it in so it wouldn't blow apart.

June filled up pitchers and carried them over her head, waiting on tables, slipping money into her apron. There were more college kids than she'd expected, and more men in orange hats and down vests than she'd ever seen in one place in her life, but it was the college kids that started the chant and she knew that because the people who were used to Klemper's Bar hadn't ever said anything the same and coordinated in their whole lives.

"What are they yelling?" Otto asked, grabbing her sleeve when she went by, and she knew he'd turned his hearing aid off and was losing his "t's."

"They want tits," she said, talking right in his face.

Somebody knocked her arm then and crashed a pitcher and beer glasses on the floor and the new noise, the brittle crash and skid of glass and the yells that answered it, pushed up the volume so it was like some animal energy in the bar. June wondered if the roof would stay on. Maybe it was deer hunting fever, she thought, crunching herself against people and sweeping up glass. Maybe that was part of it, the thing in a man and a deer people say is ready to burst when they find each other. Maybe it was a feeling like that, which was cranked up and shut in tight inside her bar with all the noise.

June looked at the clock and wondered if it was right, if something about this noise speeded up time. It was seven thirty, a half an hour to go. She hoped they'd ordered enough beer.

Fifteen minutes later word came the girls were in the back getting ready. June didn't have a clue how Charlie had gotten them in, but a roar went through the crowd. There were people climbing on the tables and on each other's shoulders and there were still men coming in the door. Somebody had crushed Otto's Tab in the middle and got his shirt soaked and June thought he should go home, but Tarr Hansen had a grip on his shoulder and was talking to him, all red-eyed, and June had a whole line and backfield blocking her away from them. Everything smelled like beer. The floor smelled like beer and she wondered if the air could catch fire from pure alcohol.

"Where are they?" she heard Tarr bellow. He was holding on to Otto's shoulder and his tongue was thick like he had to push the words out. "They were my girls—one of mine I'd strap her. Otto, you find the john?"

By the time it was eight, June thought the girls could have floated out to the bar. There was enough beer on the floor to start a river and the music going didn't have a thing to do with solid earth. It was all steam and heat and she'd never heard so many people breathing except maybe once when her father's best friend threatened to kill himself in front of a whole crowd and she heard people not breathing. And then the girls were there. The door to the back room was open and the crowd was snaking where they came through with everybody yelling, and they were all flesh and blood and done-up hair and, one by one, they were raised up and lifted onto the bar.

June stood on her tiptoes and took a look at what she'd hired. There were six girls in thong underpants and tight T-shirts and three of them had long hair pinned back with flowers and four were blondes. They were doing these dances up on the bar, bending a little at the knees and shaking or doing this slow, dying pivot of their hips with their hands up in the air, and June thought maybe that's what bringing the house down meant, because the floor was heaving and she thought for sure the ceiling beams would cave in. There was screaming and whistling so she thought her eardrums would break and then Charlie's announcer turned on the microphone and it started to shriek and five hundred people were yelling for water for the shirts, and the announcer dragged the microphone wire across the bar so that one girl tripped and nearly fell. The whole crowd seemed to lurch forward and hands were grabbing over the bar at the girls' ankles and legs.

It was Reed who moved them back. June, filling glasses, saw him do it, but the announcer was talking then, telling the crowd to stay clear of the bar so the contest could start. June was stunned at how beautiful the girls were. And how young. Every one of them looked eighteen, in spite of her orders to Charlie they had to be twenty-one, and some of them were giggling and one seemed scared to death and another looked about too drunk to stay standing.

June watched. The ice water buckets came out and got poured down the girls, and they squealed and wiggled, and their breasts came shining up firm through their T-shirts like rose-studded softballs, and the crowd was whistling and stomping and hooting, and the air was blue from smoke and bluer from words, and June wondered if her face showed some of what she felt, that there was something unbelievable going on she almost liked, something like the creek when it flooded and you went deaf listening and watched all the foam and the thick color in the water.

She hunted for Reed and couldn't find him. There were men yelling so their eyes bulged, and the beer and sweat oozing down them and all those red faces and the way the crowd seemed to move together like a pump handle pressing down and then flying loose. The girl who was the new Miss Runner-Up had lost her T-shirt altogether and the drunk girl was putting money in her underpants for some hunter to hunt for. She'd upstaged the statuesque blonde the announcer said was Miss Klemper's Bar, and it was Josie's Bill that roared up to the bar to claim the money. *Josie's husband, Bill.* June couldn't believe it. She wanted to grab him and pitch him over the bar, and then Otto was standing next to her, his breath coming short and she got him outside, past all the faces that she memorized as she went by, looking at them hard like she'd found out something new: her eyes stripped clear into seeing.

"Can you breathe, Otto?" she said and when she knew he could, she let his hand go and sucked her own breath in. "They're stupid," she said. "Those girls." She was trembling, yelling, yelling over the music and into Otto's deafness. "They're stupid. I'm stupid. We all are. We don't anyone admit you all hate us."

"Simmer down, June." Otto had her by the arms.

"It's true. You men all hate us." June was crying, and Otto shook his head.

"It's not that easy. No, honey. I told you how my unit in the war got panicked pushing too far into unsecured territory? It's like that, June. People get different when they're way out front."

"Screw your philosophy, Otto. You go home now. Go. You want me to walk you home?"

"I'm all right. I'm going," Otto said, and June watched him head up the road past all the cars, and she went into the house through the back door and called the sheriff to come close the bar early.

Which is what he did, though not before the whole place was a wreck. It was a shambles, really, and the word was afterward that Klemper's was done having promotions whether June got ambitious some more or not. Somebody said the cleanup and repairs and fine were ten thousand dollars—more—and that was the tame part of the wild talk that went on for weeks.

After a while, though, the stories tapered off, died down a little, maybe from politeness, maybe from something murkier, more uncertain. Yet there was still a feeling, a sense of residue from the contest like the rings that spread out thinner in the water from a stone's throw or what they say stays in the body from radiation.

Reed painted out the letters under the bar sign the very next morning. But awhile back, the "Home" started to bleed through so you can see it, which is strange, people think, with June long gone—she and the kids in Arizona now, June selling real estate with her mother and settled there for good.

At Flood Tide

Overnight the change began. The wind blew and blew, humming at the outside corners of the house like a shaking guitar string, and by morning the sky was clear, the air mild, and the snow that lay in a stiff triangle below the northern slope started to crack. When the sun shone, brown creases ran everywhere and snow sank in pools into the earth. At noon the creek had swollen to the height of its banks and was racing hard through the valley, hissing along like a giant snake.

Franklin Gage eyed it, listening. A tall man, he looked even taller at the top of the hill above the creek, for he stood with the rigor of a watched guard. He was wearing a khaki jacket and black hip waders, yet he gave an overall impression of a calm and elegant grayness. It came in part from his graying hair and gray-flecked beard, but more from the feeling one got in looking at him that his best suits, his favorite sweater, his car, and his dog would all be gray.

In spite of this appearance he made of coolness, Franklin Gage was in a state of some excitement. In five years of weekend trips to his country farmhouse, he had never seen the creek flood, and although he felt his morning vigil and his solitary trip the night before to start the fire and turn on the water in the house had earned him the right to have the scene to himself, he wished (rather sharply, he realized) that Amanda, his wife, would arrive soon so she wouldn't miss it. Amanda was the one, after all, who watched the place by seasons, jotting down frost dates and bird migrations, rainfall, the color of caterpillars, the sites of trillium and jack-in-the-pulpit and snakeroot. Of the two of them, she was the informed, the natural naturalist.

Franklin unbuttoned his jacket. There were the two Amandas, of course—Amanda the sophisticate who seemed always carefully and freshly arranged—just dressed in something tailored or muted but iridescent, wonderful with her hair shining and pulled slightly back at one ear so the hoop of her earring showed—the Amanda who conquered guests with perfect food and better wit and who claimed she liked the people here because they seemed original, but who actually, he knew, liked them because the garbagemen and loggers, the caretaker, and the farmers up and down the road had all fallen in love with her.

To him, that Amanda had a hint of artifice at times, a suggestion of uncertainty and self-consciousness. But the other Amanda, who could work until midnight readying her gallery for a show and be up at dawn to start work again, the Amanda who had raised her sons with a kind of diligent prescience and who kept a weekend almanac, had a capacity for absorption which seemed somehow to defy the notion of self. That was the Amanda who, if she hurried now, would see the flood and who, in a sense, would keep it for them.

Franklin started down the hill toward the creek. Whitewater was pounding in the current and where rivulets of water ran into the creek a muddy foam had backed up on the snow. It was the start, he realized, of the flood. Water spread out suddenly across the land, moving forward in an irregular curve, its course like the path of an army staggered in its advance by terrain. Franklin tried to hear the water as an army, as a racket of tanks and mortars and screaming men and falling bodies all fused into a giant roar, but it stayed in his mind instead—thunderously, insistently—as water. And now there were other sounds, too—the scolding worry of a flock of birds circling on the hillside and the faint sound of his own name called down to him.

He turned around. Amanda was at the top of the hill. She waved and he crunched through the snow, climbing up the hill to her.

"There's your flood," he said. He kissed her. "It's a river. Did you sell anything?"

"It wasn't a client."

"Well you're here," Franklin said. There was a strained note in Amanda's voice, but he let it go. "Come on down. It's like all the fountains in Italy when you're closer to it."

"Are we skiing? We're not skiing. I'll have to change. Ah—look at him! My God, it's a crane, isn't it—or a heron?"

An enormous blue bird with beating wings had come in low over the creek and seemed ready to land. It hesitated but then kept going, flapping away to the trees. "A heron," Amanda said. Her voice was quiet and Franklin could barely hear her over the noise of the water.

"You know what all that reminds me of?" he asked.

"You said Italy."

"Besides that. The water, being on the water, going into Dun Laoghaire with the gulls flying at ship's speed—"

". . . and the hills white in the mist and the sun's rays streaking through clouds and into the water. Why haven't we gone back?"

"It's reminded me of that whole trip. The whole year. What it reminded me of was you."

Amanda laughed. She slipped her hand along her neck and then looked at him.

"You remember that summer?"

"Of course." She was quiet, staring again at the creek, and Franklin knew they were in the same place, on a broad back stairs in the Victoria and Albert Museum with him going up to hunt for tiles and her sitting on a step looking at the ceiling. It was the first time he had seen her, twelve years before, and he had remembered forever after that she had looked like a woman who was attached in all the important places—to a man, to a family and work and her own history, and that he had liked that apprehension of her as fully a woman and settled, and had needed only the startling information that there was no man, that he had died in Vietnam, in order to take his attraction to her seriously.

"What's England full of?" she said, her eyes still on the creek.

"Loot. What do the English attack with on the stairway to the Tube?"

"Umbrellas. What can't they live without?"

"Queuing. Secret—no, official sin."

They were both laughing, but then Amanda turned back toward the house. "I'm tired. The traffic was bad. I think I'll read," she said, and there was an edge to her voice again that seemed to warn him away.

For the rest of the afternoon, Franklin occupied himself watching the creek and cutting dead branches for firewood. He had traded his hip waders for work boots, and the melted snow seeping through the leather made his feet feel as damp to him as all of England. Everything, suddenly, reminded him of England. The sky was blue, but the creek crashed along as impudently as the ocean bumped up on the pier in Brighton. His toes squished as they always did in England where he'd even abandoned his bachelorhood with wet feet instead of cold ones, his shoes squeaking as he ran up the steps to the flat where Amanda's friends lived—the standard English artist's flat, she said, with white walls and paper globes on the light fixtures—and got married in a room filled with roses from the garden and with Amanda's small sons in attendance, both dressed in short pants.

It had been, he thought, as daring a thing as he had ever done, giving up at thirty-seven the carefully nurtured habits of his single life. He had always expected that he would do it sometime. In fact, he had had a scenario in mind, complete with a previously disposed of first husband (he'd never quite thought to kill him off), to make the match, in his view, more liable to steadiness. He had wanted a woman who was over the rough spots, clear about who she was and what she needed, and Amanda had suited perfectly. What had surprised him, though, was how abruptly she became essential to him and how, at times, he had an unsettling feeling of pain when he looked at the long muscles of her thighs and the faint stretch marks on her breasts and saw them as records, in some way important, of a life that preceded him.

Franklin carried the last of the wood he had cut across the yard and put it in the shed. The thin rifts the sun had made in the snow were muddy swaths now that cut everywhere into the hillsides and far edges of the valley. The creek had settled into a new course, sweeping urgently along through the center of the valley and hurling felled branches into stranded trees in a kind of dumb show in which the noise of the impact was suffocated by the water. The water covered every sound. Even the whir of the chain saw that ragged at his mind was muted by its boom. He did not think he could escape it. He was not sure even that he wanted to, and his eyes searched across the water, hunting for something, for anything unexpected.

What he found instead was the shimmer of sunlight, bouncing from the water and mirrored back to him, to the image that had stayed in his mind, of Amanda and her long thighs and her breasts with their tiny pitted marks that disappeared when she moved. He took his jacket from the tree branch and went inside to find her.

"Amanda?" He started up the stairs.

There was a movement in the dining room, and she had answered him before he started back down. "In here."

He looked in the doorway. She was standing at the window, gazing out at the creek, and she was wearing a dress he'd never seen before that looked like rainbows sewn together. "We're going out?" he said. There was something in the line of her back that made her seem as unapproachable now as she had earlier.

"I didn't buy groceries," she answered.

"You're smoking."

She looked at him and then back out the window. "Should we get reservations?"

"You're hungry now?"

"No. Impatient." She turned around, cigarette in hand, and her eyes darted at him and across the room. "I feel like being somewhere else."

"I like your dress," he said. He waited a minute longer, looking at her. Then, feeling that he was denying himself, being denied, he went upstairs to the bedroom to change.

When they left for the restaurant, the gas gauge in Amanda's car was nearly on empty. Franklin pulled into a SuperAmerica at the edge of town and checked the wiper fluid and oil while the tank filled. The snow was melting here, too. He watched a patch of it slide off the roof of the station and crumple with a thud as it hit the dumpster. Inside, he paid with a credit card and picked up a copy of the local newspaper which Amanda read for the "Serenity News" and "Sooner Saunters," the full accounting of the week's visits in blink-sized towns she didn't know a soul in, though she had learned well enough what people were friends with one another.

"Am I a snob?" she always asked Franklin. "Is that the pleasure in it?"

"Maybe," he told her, though it was usually at a certain hour of a certain kind of social evening when they'd insisted to acquaintances that they'd stayed in Minneapolis—the place they'd picked to live after London because Amanda wouldn't go back to San Francisco and because he was tired of the perpetual sense of the outsider that lingered with him in New York and because Minneapolis dangled the job for him, a lot of money in the business end of the theater—stayed only because its food conglomerates and Dayton-Hudson (the corporate force behind the spread of the bookstore chain) made it the actual center of the nation's stomach and reduced collective mind.

Mornings after that kind of night Amanda always said she felt morally sullied. "We're awful," she'd call after him when he went off to find the aspirin bottle. "And don't ever let me read the 'Serenity News' again."

Franklin signed the credit card slip and got his card back and went outside. He opened the car door and, as he got in, felt the rush of warm air from the heater. "Here's your paper," he said, holding it out to Amanda.

She shook her head. "I don't want it," she answered and her voice was husky, dark, almost as if she'd been crying.

"You OK?" he asked.

A pickup, waiting for the gas pump, flashed its lights behind them. Franklin looked in the mirror and turned the key in the ignition. He pulled the car over to the edge of the asphalt and pushed the gearshift into neutral. "What's the matter?" he said.

Amanda hugged her jacket collar up around her and stared at the windshield. She wasn't crying. Not exactly. She seemed to be collecting herself. "I don't think I'm up for a restaurant."

"You want me to buy something?"

"Here?"

"Dried out chicken. Spam. Amanda, what's wrong?"

He waited.

Finally she cleared her throat. "Nothing. I'm just upset. Nothing happened. Not really. I told you it wasn't a client this morning. I got caught off guard."

Alarmed, Franklin looked at her. "You didn't get mugged?"

"Nothing like that. This is silly. There was this printmaker from Los Angeles Joe Speers sent."

"So?"

"He reminded me of Peter."

"Peter?"

"*Peter.*" Her voice had gotten higher, and Franklin quickly nodded his head. Peter. Her first husband's name had been Peter.

"He didn't really look like him—well, maybe something about the way his eyes were set. But he was the age Peter would be, and his work was exactly what Peter's would be if he were still alive."

"That's a big guess."

"It's not. It was this uncanny thing. It was like an assault."

"What did you do?"

"I told him to leave. I said we weren't that kind of gallery. When he was gone, I sat there shaking for an hour."

Franklin shifted the car into gear and pulled out onto the road. He turned back in the same direction they'd come.

Amanda looked at him, then out the window into the darkness. "Where are we going?" she asked.

"Klein's. We can eat in the corner. You can have a drink. We'll be invisible."

"You hate their food."

"I cut two cords of wood. I'll eat anything." Franklin reached over, feeling for Amanda's hand, touching it before she moved it away. "I'm sorry you were so upset," he said. "I've got a new one for your list." He was thinking of her discoveries: Balzac's tell it to the marines; outta sight from Frank Norris in *McTeague*. Last night he'd stumbled on James himself in *The Ambassadors*.

"Looking out for number one," he said.

He waited. He waited listening, but Amanda was quiet.

At the county road he turned south, heading for Klein's, and wondered if the creek was still flooded. He was trying to sort through what he knew about Peter Gaines, the history Amanda had given him, which had been necessary of course, but, in his view, mercifully succinct. She'd met him in college. A New England town. A campus with broad greens, brick buildings, shade trees to lie under. She'd been the decorous art history student and he the artist in the studio. The real thing, she said. They'd gotten married after graduation, traveled until the draft felt too ominous. Then he'd screwed up. In the second year of graduate school in San Francisco he took a shortcut through a line at registration and missed the card for the draft board. *Boom*: 1-A. They couldn't get it undone. They'd had David and she was pregnant with Josh when he left for Vietnam, and she was pregnant after they met for his R&R in Hawaii, though she lost that baby. Peter, she'd told him, had thought it was a girl. She had thought so herself.

Franklin had offered a polite question when she finished her story. "He wanted a daughter?" he asked. Amanda had nodded, answered yes.

Now as she twisted at her necklace, her neck curving away from him as she looked out the window, Franklin thought dimly of the other question, the obvious one that had not seemed obvious before. Had she wanted a daughter, too, Peter's daughter but not his?

He eased into a curve, reminded himself of what he'd always believed, that Amanda had not wanted more children, that like him she had found their family comfortably complete. He had been a father to the boys—a reliable ride, a reliable checkbook. He enjoyed them, loved them, thought they loved him. When occasionally he heard Amanda telling them about trekking with Peter in Nepal before they were born or saying Peter had told her the only sounds he could hear when his unit flew into Vietnam were the plane's engines and soldiers crying, he found her stories quite moving.

But he did not himself have any information about this man to give to their sons. He and Amanda never discussed him. He believed, too, that she did not talk about him with anyone else and, though it was nothing he would ever say to her, he assumed it was from embarrassment somehow, that she considered it the wrong subject for their friends. Draft dodgers.

But he was missing something now. Why was she so distressed after all these years?

Franklin turned on his blinker and waited for a truck to go by before he pulled into Klein's. There was an airplane high overhead on the flight path that followed the creek valley. It was a lone light threading across the dark sky, a solitary presence here though it was headed for traffic, the noisy descent into the hubbub and energy of the city at night.

"You know the Vietnam thing," he said, thinking out loud. "The war? I never thought you should feel guilty he was there. Embarrassed or whatever. He got stuck with it like a lot of people. Unlucky devil, though."

Franklin stopped. Amanda was staring at him. She looked completely astonished and he was suddenly at a loss for what to say. He sat with his hands on the steering wheel. Then he shifted himself, got out. He opened Amanda's side of the car and waited. The Leinenkugel's sign blinked a "g" at them from Klein's front window.

He stood with the car door open. Finally, whitely still, Amanda stepped out of the car. She grasped her skirt away from the water pooled in the parking lot, crossed the broken asphalt to Klein's door.

Inside she sat in her jacket at a corner table while he ordered at the bar. He came back with a whiskey for her, a beer for himself.

"Art says hello," he said, but she didn't look up, didn't nod at Art Klein behind the bar. Instead she pulled her jacket tighter.

"You're cold?" Franklin asked.

"I thought you promised invisibility," she answered, and he was relieved. Finally her voice.

"It's pretty close," he said. "You know anybody here besides Art?"

"Tarr Hansen's here. Rick Stosser's here. Pretty soon Lloyd Thomas'll show up and they'll have euchre night."

"It's not Wednesday. I ordered you a hamburger. It was that or leftovers from the liver feed."

"Franklin—"

He tried another tack. "If it's all slush tomorrow, what would you like to do? We could take a drive. We could go out at dawn and drive up and down the street in—what's the name of it? Winnow."

She didn't answer but she was with him, he thought—in the small, damp town in the gray morning with wind-bells chiming on what used to be the front of the tourist home.

"How could you ever have thought that?" she said.

"About Winnow?"

"Not Winnow. That I was embarrassed! God. Embarrassed. You think I'm embarrassed the man I was married to was killed in Vietnam?"

Franklin looked at the pool table by the windows where a girl was high-fiving her boyfriend over a perfect bank shot. "Well, not that exactly," he said. He made his way slowly. "But everybody we ever met was a peace marcher or a draft evader. I thought you'd find it awkward. You know—dragging out his Purple Heart or whatever. That kind of thing."

"You could say that? I don't believe this. I don't believe we're having this conversation." Amanda was reaching for her purse. She picked it up, then put it back down abruptly and pulled her jacket off. "You're right. We'll eat," she said. "And listen. Franklin, listen. I thought I was doing you a favor in not talking about Peter—except to the boys, of course—but if that's the idea you've gotten I've made a horrible mistake. Horrendous."

Amanda stopped, waited while Sue Klein put their food down, waited while Sue set out their silverware and talked about the flood knocking out the sump pump so there was five feet of water under the part of the bar that had a basement. She was worried about snakes.

When she finally left, Amanda looked at him and, with the bad light, he couldn't tell if she had tears in her eyes. "I'm not done. He never talked about the war. He censored it out of his letters. He gave me pictures instead. Sometimes in words. Sometimes real drawings. Sometimes in color."

Franklin was careful. "Like what?"

"Lots of green." Amanda held her forehead with her hand, her elbow on the table. "Blue thatched roofs. A faded, rose-colored jacket on a peasant woman. The back of her. Shadows in the folds of the cloth."

"In the delta?"

"In the jungle. In the delta. In villages. I could always see where he was. There was this ropy thinness in the old men he sketched. And I had the shapes of leaves and tree bark. Straw. Rice paddies. He left out his friends. I think it was superstition—that if he drew them it was something final, a picture of record.

"And looking at that work Joe sent today . . . it stunned me. Absolutely. I saw how much I've not even imagined what our lives would have been. I think Peter knew he wouldn't come back. That he was handing his life to somebody else to live. Minus the pictures, minus who he was alone, that would be you."

Franklin absorbed this, leaned back mentally from the sucker punch. "That would be me," he said. "Minus the theater. Minus who I am alone. You want me to get you another drink?"

Amanda pushed back from the edge of the table, pivoted her toes to work her shoes back on. "Let's go home," she said, and Franklin helped her with her jacket, left money for the bill and tip beside her untouched food.

Outside he smelled the moistness of the air, heard the booming of the creek. "I don't like it," Amanda said. "An early spring. It won't last. We'll hate the rest of winter."

Franklin opened the car door for her. He got in on his side and started the motor and they drove in silence to the darkest stretch of the creek road. He flashed his bright lights on and slowed down for the last curve before their driveway.

"What would it be like," Amanda said when he'd parked the car, "if all of them smashed their security lights?" She was looking off across the distance at the green lights that dotted the countryside. "We'd have a wilderness," she answered her own question. "We'd be at the ends of the earth."

"The creek's still flooded," he said. He hesitated and then touched her arm. "Walk down with me? I'm sorry about what I said. All of it. I wasn't thinking. 'Looking out for number one.' *The Ambassadors*," he said quickly, realizing he'd confused her, mixed the content and form of what he'd said. "I found it last night," he told her, and she nodded, then answered his first question.

"Not in these shoes. It's too cold anyway. But maybe . . . OK." She turned in the direction of the creek and he watched her dress float out below her jacket, her hair move over her shoulders as she walked.

"You coming?" she called, looking back at him. "We need a sled."

Franklin followed her. "It wouldn't budge," he said. "Put your weight forward so your heels don't sink."

"What if I get stuck in this snow and muck and the temperature drops and I freeze to death?"

"You could take your shoes off and escape instead."

"I like these shoes." Amanda put her hands in her pockets and started off down the hillside, walking easily, as he knew she would, as sure-footed as a mountain goat.

He said her name, but the noise of the creek had taken over.

"What?" She looked back at him. He shook his head and pointed at the sky of stars and scattered clouds that had moved in from the west and rolled swiftly across the moon.

"It's so dark and so light," Amanda said. She spoke in his ear when he reached her. They were closer to the water now and the sound of it came at them with different voices—frontally, obliquely, a reedy clatter from the west and, to the east, a dying, black tumble of sound falling away into the woods.

"I think I forgive you," she said, raising her arms to him, and he reached his hands around her under her jacket, and he wanted to make love to her with the rush of water pounding in his ears, with even a chilly crust of snow pushing up between them.

But she had gone abruptly rigid against him.

"There," she whispered. He half twisted, looking over his shoulder where she was staring at the thin island of land that lay now between two channels of water. The heron was there, his wings hunched back along his body, one leg bent and poised. He was there watching them. Then he moved, straightened his leg, dipped his beak into the water. He lifted his head and, lumbering into the sky, he flew away.

"You think he lives here?" Franklin asked, but Amanda had pushed away from him and was going quickly down the hillside. Franklin hesitated, waiting for her to turn back.

"What're you doing?" he called. She'd reached the water's edge. She was pulling her shoes off, and she held her skirt up so the bottom of her hem drifted out along the water.

"Amanda!" he yelled.

She didn't stop. She was in the water up to her waist, up to her neck. And then, in spite of his headlong crash down the hillside, before he could reach her, before he could save her, she had thrashed and scrambled her way back onto the land.

"Amanda," he said. "What in the world?" She was coughing, panting a little. She was like an eel in his arms. He wrung the water out of her skirt, tried pulling her shoes on.

"Dammit," she said. She was shivering, and the water came off her like water from a shaking dog. He tugged at her shoe strap.

"Let's go up. Come on," he said, his arm tight around her. She was coughing and drenched.

"No. Not yet. Not yet." She stood with her shoes half on and her lips trembling. "Franklin, not this ever again. No floods, no more giant birds in the night. I didn't marry you for that." Her mouth had gone purple, and she was hanging on to his jacket sleeve. "I can't bear it. I can't live that way again. All the intensity. All the miraculous wildness."

Franklin heard her, saw the distortion of her face, felt the words enter him and rive through.

"Let's go," he said once more. He was pushing, half carrying her up the hill, his arm and whole shoulder soaked where he held her around the waist, and he was reaching in his mind for the light they had left burning by the kitchen sink, for the heat radiating from the stove, for what he could say that wasn't agreement.

Amanda's teeth chattered and her wet skirt rasped against her knees. She was crying now.

"All right," Franklin said. "All right, Amanda," In the noise of the dark, he thought he heard the creek diminish. Fall quiet. That it receded now, inch by inch, into its banks.

Anthony Martin Is Dead

It was said there was a question of foul play. It was true the boy was not a strong swimmer. He was barely a swimmer at all, having come from the kind of family where lessons in swimming, in tennis and piano, are not a part of growing up. In fact, he was hardly a boy. At seventeen he had pushed at manhood, his body already lengthened and broadened toward full maturity.

There was no suggestion that what had happened was planned. There was no alleged grudge, no rivalry over a girl. If, in the end, Anthony Martin had not been stretched out blue and dead on the sand, the afternoon's events might have seemed no more remarkable than those of other summer days when the customary horseplay threatens, for a time, to go too far. But there was a body on the sand and there was the whole chain of mourning and recrimination it predicted and so the day was not like any other.

The place where Anthony Martin lay until the rescue team abandoned its efforts and the ambulance drove silently back to town, was at the busiest part of the riverbank, a place where the summer's traffic in fishermen and picnickers and teenagers had worn away all but a handful of the grass tufts that sprouted from the sand. It was the smoothest place to put a body, but it was only happenstance that Anthony Martin lay there, for the spot was directly above the point where he had finally been pulled from the river. The gouge his body had made in the sand as it was dragged across the embankment was clearly visible.

By the time the body was covered and placed inside the ambulance, what had been an uproar of screams and sirens, slamming doors and shouted directions, had died utterly away. There was absolute quiet. One of the teenagers who had been Anthony Martin's companions on his last swim sat twisted with her legs to the side and her face pressed against the tire of a car when the ambulance drew away. Another lay facedown on the sand, almost without breathing. The boys were edgy, standing at a kind of half attention, and while they watched the ambulance leave, one of them tugged at his swimsuit, trying to stretch it higher.

In all, there were maybe a dozen of them, a handful of girls, the rest boys, and none of them, in talking earlier to the policeman who was writing now on a clipboard in the front seat of his squad car, had claimed to be a friend of Anthony Martin.

"Sue knows him," one boy said, and a tall blonde girl who was standing at his right had shrugged her shoulders so the mole at the top of her bathing suit had lifted a full inch toward her chin.

"In grade school," she said.

No, none of them were really his friends. It was said, in fact, that Anthony Martin was not the sort of boy who easily made friends. It was not an instinct he had or a skill he had learned, though a person observing him could not have seen if he found this lack a shortcoming in himself. In this regard and in others, he was not an easy boy to read, having shown since childhood an apparent dullness of emotion. No one knew if the ridicule he suffered for failure at games, his slowness in school, had left a scar, or how it was he had become who he was of the loved, sweet-smelling children of the first day of kindergarten.

But maybe this for a start: *In the room a lady bends over saying hello hello. She has orange hair. She smells like cranberry sauce and has glasses that smell like metal. She bends over more, asking your name. "He goes by Anthony," your mother says, and the windows are open. There is a round place with carpet and another place with tables and small chairs and pictures that go up to the ceiling and gerbils in a cage. You like Oscar best. He is brown in his fur and eyes and does not scamper on your arm. He is smooth like a large egg with something happening inside. He belongs to the letter "O" on the wall above the pencil sharpener. When it is time to sit on the carpet, the lady puts Oscar back in the cage. It is the rule for him to go, but Oscar bites the orange hair, and that makes you glad.*

Or maybe this: *At recess you run for the ball. A foot hooks between your legs and kicks the ball away. You fall. You fall, too, from the monkey bars and the black tar puts blood on your nose. It is a rule that you don't cross the street to go home. You can follow your sneakers and shadow next to the sidewalk, next to the grass until the bell rings and the lady puts paper towels and cold water on your nose. The water drips and you cover your pants that are wet where you pee, though you didn't . . .*

Maybe those things, though maybe not. With Anthony Martin's body cooling in its seal of blankets and the ambulance turning onto the bridge, if no one could say, no one could know.

"We're going over it once more," the policeman ordered. He had put down his clipboard and gotten out of the car. "You were there." He walked over to the group and pointed a little way down the river where two other officers were taking measurements along the bank. "And some of you decided to swim over to the other side, and on the way the Martin boy went down, and six of you diving took ten minutes to get him out. Anybody got something to add to that?"

There was quiet still. One boy, who was shivering slightly, opened a car door and picked up a T-shirt from the back of the seat and pulled it on, but no one said anything.

"Grubaker—you're a lifeguard, right?" The policeman was pointing his pencil at a smallish, well-muscled boy with a chip off his front tooth. Then he looked around. "How many good swimmers here? Ten minutes is a long time."

"I tried to help but he was panicked, choking me." The girl next to the car tire almost lunged to her feet. Her voice was shrill. "I got loose and he was gone." Her voice was shaking, and one of the boys pulled her backward, pulled her against his chest and held her there while she trembled.

The policeman looked at them before he went on. "And the rest of you? What were you—twenty feet from the bank? Twenty feet!" His voice had gone shrill, too, and he wheeled around and went back to his car. He put in a call on the radio.

When he returned, he stared at the river without speaking. "All right, you can go," he said finally. "Write down your names and addresses and then go. All of you just go home."

He set his jaw and when the last car engine had gunned its way up the road, the officer drove across town and listened to Anthony Martin's mother screaming in her apron as he stood on the doorstep in front of her.

As it turned out, there were not so many people who remembered even knowing Anthony Martin. "He was the redheaded kid, or was he the skinny kid with the cycle?" his barber asked, and more than one of Anthony Martin's high school teachers did not make the right connection between name and face until they'd hunted through the school yearbook.

Even among the family it seemed there was a certain vagueness in apprehending who he was. That he had been theirs, flesh and blood, was sure. They knew, too, that in all his life he would have kept a particular burliness and high color and have moved with a forward incline to his walk.

But they did not understand what kind of man he would have been. They knew the things he had liked—flannel shirts and magazines with pictures of cars—but they did not know if the occasional willfulness that had shown itself as he grew older would have hardened into a wild streak, a pleasure in doing something wrong.

Nor was it clear to the family what this son could have done for a life's work. He had learned from his father how to trap, how to panel a basement room, but he had neither the patience nor, with his thick hands, the dexterity for his father's finer sort of carpentry.

"Maybe the army," his father said at the funeral home, talking to no one in particular, letting the words trail away.

"He looks real nice. Such a tall boy," people said, looking at Anthony Martin lying in his coffin with an unaccustomed tie knotted at his neck, the usual blush of his skin painted on by hand, and it seemed that those were the words that gave some comfort to his mother. She would look at him, her eyes traveling fitfully over his body, her hands twitching at a strand of hair, a smoothed lapel, and her face would go soft as if she still had the scent of him from babyhood in her nostrils.

Yet if there was no clear sense of what Anthony Martin had been or would become, there was a growing awareness in town that his name was not unfamiliar, that it had been heard in another context—a recent involvement in an accident, nearly fatal, in which someone had been drunk, someone had been jailed, though not Anthony Martin.

The police officer, whose name was Peterson Reisack, woke up on the first night after Anthony Martin's death with the connection suddenly gripping him, and in the morning he went to work before his shift to check the records from a month before, to do the police work of investigation that could ease his mind, ease him, the father of three, back from the shock that recoiled on him like a rifle blast, the shock that had stayed with him since he had watched the body into the blankets.

He read through the accident report, made a sketch for himself and then matched it to the reporting officer's diagram and photos of the scene. Early a.m. accident. Three vehicles, three young male drivers, one of them drunk and cited and charged. Anthony Martin the innocent perpetrator, his car traveling on the highway from the north and striking a vehicle propelled from an idling stop through a T-intersection by a car that slammed it from the rear. Tread marks. Measurements. Not a chance for the Martin boy to stop though he had swerved enough to deflect the impact, to save, it would seem, a young man's life. And the upshot five weeks later: one person in jail, one still in the hospital, and the third, by coincidence, now in the morgue.

Officer Reisack xeroxed everything for his own file. Case to be closed with the medical examiner's report. Or, possibly, case pending.

The obituary for Anthony Martin was brief. Besides his parents, it said, he was survived by an older brother and twin nieces, a younger sister, and one grandmother who had relocated to Tempe in Arizona for her health. He had aunts and uncles, numerous cousins, and he was being buried from Holy Peace Lutheran Church, with services at 11 a.m. on Saturday. There was no suggestion for memorials, no mention of any high school activities Anthony Martin had participated in, for the family had drawn a blank when the question was asked. A grainy photograph of a young Scout with a trophy accompanied the article and, seeing it, the secretary of the photographer who was scheduled to take Anthony Martin's senior picture in two weeks made a note to herself to cancel his appointment.

It was Anthony Martin's father who had supplied the photograph, taking it from his wallet and placing it on the counter in the newspaper office. "I'll want it back," he said to the reporter he gave it to, and he was still waiting at the counter when she returned from a story an hour later.

"We'll mail it to you. Or you could pick it up Monday," she told him, thinking as she spoke that grief makes a man small, that it strips away the bearing which gives him his size.

At the funeral home, the father seemed to feel the empty place in his wallet as another loss. He kept touching his pocket, inhaling sharply at the memory of his son with his pinebox car and at the thought of himself slapping and cursing a young son for clumsiness. He had finished the car alone in his shop, built a winner, but in a whole night of studying the picture of his son he had not been able to see that Anthony minded. He was smiling. He had a trophy.

And maybe it was like this: *They snap a picture of you because your car that was a block of wood is best and everybody knows. You touch the shiny red paint, twirl the wheels and feel the balance of the car's slight ounces in your hand. The cars are sleek flying down the track and your car is always fastest, always the one to gain speed at the end. You pick it up, laugh that you've won, stomp your feet, laugh that everyone knows this car is yours . . .*

In town it was said the police were making additional inquiries, that Officer Reisack had talked once more to everyone whose name was on his list, that he had spoken to the man who was serving a sentence for reckless endangerment in the accident that compressed the vertebrae in the injured man's back, had spoken to that man as well, and to various family members until some people were wondering, really wondering if there was a plot afoot to harm the name of innocent kids, to pile more tragedy on top of what already was.

Yet it was said, too, that the investigation went nowhere. That nobody knew one another, that though Anthony Martin's part in the car accident was now well known to every high school student, the injured man and the jailed man hadn't the remotest connection to anyone who had been in the water when Anthony Martin died, that Officer Reisack had told his superiors there was no case, that for all his efforts to find a connection between the two accidents, there wasn't a link he could make.

But one question remained, a question that tantalized and sifted its way through the town. Why was Anthony Martin *there*? Why was he at the river with people who were not his friends?

"It's a free country," the girl said who had gone to grade school with Anthony Martin and had seen him die. "He was just there. Like he thought we should care or something."

"I don't know why," Anthony Martin's sister told her best friend. "It was like he was swelled up after the car crash. Like he thought he was famous."

As it happened, the final version of events that became the dominant memory of Anthony Martin's death was a harsher account of what happened than the police report of accidental drowning and the transcription of the coroner's inquest. It was a version some people refused to listen to and a version that lent itself to embroidery, to the addition or subtraction of names. But whatever its truth, whatever its borrowings from rumor and speculation, it was a story whose essence survived, calling up the muggy dog days of August and a riverbank crowded with young and golden bodies and enough litter of old beer cans to put tails on the bridal cars of a whole county's worth of summer weddings, the *chee-chee* call of birds curling south above the river, the quick slap of water as a diver jackknifes off the highest point of the bank, and as he surfaces, his head tilted back so that his hair is smooth against his scalp, hoots and catcalls from the sand, a tussle there, a boy trying to pin a laughing girl against her towel, oiled shoulders beading up with water, the crunch of yellow taco wrappers and the long buzz of a locust and all at once, at the slow approach of a blue pickup, a palpable silence.

"What's he doing here?"

From the windshield, from the inside looking out across the steering wheel, the view would have been all staring eyes tracking the movement of the truck as it rolled to a stop in the dirt beyond the road.

"Hey, Martin, what are you doing here?"

But the boy in the swimming suit who gets out of the truck, an open Coke can in his hand, doesn't answer. He watches back, leaning against the cab, a kind of thick-skinned smile pushing at the corners of his mouth.

"Hey, Martin, I said what are you doing here?"

"Ignore him."

"Ignore him and maybe he'll disappear."

There is a single splash as a girl dives from the bank in a perfect arc. The scuffle on the beach towel starts again and a ball, raining drops of water, sails back and forth from a rise of land to arms waving in the river.

"Hey Martin, balance that can on your flat head."

"Hey Martin, let's see you tread that current."

"Hey Martin, we'll help you in."

He is long and reddish, flailing above the river. There is a rocketing force of water as his body hits the surface and his arms lunge out in front of him.

"Come on. Martin's going to swim the river for us."

"Look at him go. You can dunk him and he bounces back up."

"He's grinning. He likes it!"

And there is a kind of joy on Anthony Martin's face. For an instant, for longer, there is a look of glazed, almost frenzied pleasure. Then quickly it blurs. With each sputtering explosion of his head to the surface, the look grows dimmer, and when does it change at last, that great sea change to terror? The irises of his eyes are rolled back in their sockets. Water gushes from his eyelids. He is screaming, reaching and lurching with his arms . . .

But Anthony Martin is dead. All of his relatives came to the funeral and afterward sat on lawn chairs in the yard eating sandwiches and cake that the neighbors brought in.

And, now and again, when the noise of the children playing would ebb, someone glancing up could see the vacant look in the father's eyes—how the mother's hand flew in a birdlike movement to her throat and was still.

A Carnival of Animals

When the first truck came in from the freeway, it was dusk. Lights gleamed on the fast-food restaurants and the gas stations along the access road and, in the western sky, a rim of pink sank away behind the hills. It was hot out. There were girls in tank tops and halters in line at the Dairy Queen and boys stripped to the waist. Toddlers in tennis shoes and diapers held on to the straps of their mother's purses. When the trucks rolled by, everyone turned to stare at the garish pictures on the semis—of Ferris wheels and distorting mirrors—and eyed the bulging canvases that were tied down the length of the flatbed trucks.

"There's a bunch of them," said a boy at the back of the line who was a half a head taller than anyone else. The girl who was holding his hand in his back pocket nodded and brushed away the beads of sweat that glinted on her midriff.

"There's supposed to be. I heard they're having their own animals this year."

"They *are* animals," the man in front of her said, and a thin ripple of laughter ran through the line. The girl turned back from staring at the road and looked at him, but the man didn't say anything more.

Just after midnight, the last stragglers of trucks pulled through the stoplights and headed for the fairgrounds to join the camp of trucks and vans ringing the perimeter in the style of a wagon train stopped for the night. The girl, whose name was Suelinda Elly, had tiptoed past her parents' room when she came in, listening for her father to yell she was five minutes late and make her mad all over again that she had a curfew when nobody else in the whole high school did. But she heard him snoring instead, and she went on into the bathroom and washed out an ice cream stain on her halter and then got ready for bed. She crouched down in front of the open window in her bedroom. She was looking after the trucks, trying to follow the lights all the way to the fairgrounds. A mosquito hummed near her ear and then bit her in the leg and she swatted at it and thought she heard one last backing rumble of a truck in the distance. But the lights she saw now through the window were all streetlights. They were stationary, every one of them, and she pushed the covers over the end of the bed and lay down.

She was not sure, not really, what it was the man in line had meant. She'd been wondering about it and the different things that might make somebody think a person was like an animal, but the only thing that seemed very close was what Jerry Henderson had wanted her to do in his car the night before he went to the navy and even that didn't seem quite enough. She scratched her leg and straightened her nightgown behind her back. She closed her eyes. She scratched on her arm and, in a while, with her mind jumbling tattoos and broken teeth and the thick paint of grease on the gears of carnival rides, she fell asleep.

In the morning, a little after dawn, the first horse vans and livestock trucks pulled through the fairground gates. The camp was already up. There was a line of people filling containers with water at the faucet in front of the grandstand, and two children were rolling marbles in the dust and another was hanging on the door of a camper, his knees tucked up under the doorknob while he swung out over a stubble of grass. There were trucks backing into place to unload machinery for rides, and a man yelling and a noise of metal—the hard grating clash of steel on steel and a jarring ping of hammers striking nail heads. The men in the John Deere hats driving through to the animal barns drove slowly, staring through the windows of their trucks past their wives, who were pink and rounded and staring, too, to see the carnival people, to see if it was fact they were all dark and leathered sinew with muscles as hard as the metal shanks they bolted together. Gravel crunched under the wheels of the trucks and, inside the unloading pen, a pig fight started up with an enormous bellowing and squealing.

Just after nine Suelinda brought her younger brother, Joey, and the two neighbor children she watched, in through the gates to have a look. They had walked up the street pulling a wagon with a doll in it and now Daisy, the three-year-old, had climbed in on top of the doll and said her feet hurt.

"Well, I can't help it your feet hurt," Suelinda said. "You can just sit there if Joey won't pull you. Go ahead and bawl. I'm not going to listen to you." Suelinda straightened the cuffs on her shorts and squared her shoulders back. "You come on now," she said without turning around. "We get where those tractors are and you're not behaved, *you're in for it!*" She started walking slowly, waiting for the wagon to start, but she was only half listening, her real attention centered on the carnival loop where the people sitting in the dust or revving the motors on the rides had their eyes on her. She tilted her chin up and pulled her stomach tight.

"Hey there. Suelinda!" The wagon started up behind her and Suelinda looked over at the machinery display and saw her cousin Ted sitting on a spreader waving.

"Go on and talk to him, Joey," she said out of the corner of her mouth, waving back. "Tell him I got hoarse yelling at the ballgame and I got these children to take care of. Daisy, don't leave that doll in the dirt." Suelinda picked the doll up and dumped it in the wagon. "Go on, Joey," she said. She was feeling let down and cheated all at once, as if she'd been dreaming a good dream and gotten yanked awake. "How come we have to live somewhere that everybody acts like a relative—or *is*?" Suelinda took hold of Daisy with one hand and the wagon handle with the other. "Now where did Todd get to?" She shaded her eyes looking around. "Daisy, you see where your brother went?" There was a minuscule twitch started in Suelinda, like a tiny alarm bell going off, and she looked after Joey and in the farm machinery and across the road where the merry-go-round horses were all stretched out at gallop.

"There," said Daisy pointing, and Suelinda spotted him now, next to a ticket booth—Todd with the same blond curls his sister had but the longer legs, the laziness in his body. He was watching something, his weight forward on one foot as if he'd been walking somewhere and forgot to keep going.

Todd David Grenager, you trying to get yourself lost with all these strangers here? Suelinda had the words all set and she was ready to grab Todd by the waistband of his shorts and pull his heels up off the ground, but when she got to him, she tugged at his shirt without looking at it and whispered at him: "Come on, you."

There were two men standing beyond him, one she'd seen somewhere before, who had a camera around his neck, and the other a carnival man—clearly—with a giant buckle on his belt and hair that was a sheeny black like the high polish on a shoe. They were arguing, the carnival man with his eyes glaring and his hand gripping the other man's arm so it showed white.

"Come on, Todd," Suelinda whispered again, and the carnival man looked at her, his eyes dropping in an instant from her neck to the ground and then riveting back hard on the man in front of him.

"There's people here with their face in the post office that don't look to have their picture took. I said you can give me that film."

Suelinda was backing up, pulling on Todd and she pushed him and Daisy into the wagon and picked up the handle again. "If Ted's here, Uncle Ez probably is. Let's find his baby calves." She was dragging the wagon across the road, walking fast. But she couldn't get over it, the surprise of what the man had said. It was very nearly thrilling, if she knew what he'd meant, as if the newspapers and TV were coming to actual life.

"Uncle Ez, are you here?" Suelinda looked in the cow shed where the calves were tethered, and then she pulled the wagon down the middle aisle, letting Daisy and Todd rub on the calves' ears, and all the while she was wondering what it would be like for somebody with his picture in the post office, what he would have done in the line of murder or robbing banks. She was thinking of people in striped uniforms. She was thinking of a man with his head smashed into a toilet, the way she'd seen in a movie once.

In the evening, when she'd done the supper dishes, listening the whole time to her parents argue on the back porch about whose fault it was her brother was getting divorced, Suelinda went upstairs to take a shower. The fan was blowing in the hall and she stood awhile in front of it, trying to cool off. She was going back to the fairgrounds again. She had a date for 7:30 with Joel Krieke, who was pretty much her boyfriend now that Jerry Henderson had gone to the navy and her mother said she was too young to wait (Suelinda figured *she* was paying for whatever it was they thought her brother'd done wrong), and she felt halfway as if she was already there. In her room with her clothes off on the bed and her robe on and Smokey Robinson playing on the record player, she was as good as in one of those campers. With her eyes shut, she could see the flowered curtains on the window. There was a silk wrapper flung over a chair and the smell of fingernail polish and there were coffee cups with rings in them and a start of mold and ashtrays full of cigarette butts. Suelinda let her hips go back and forth, swaying to the music. They were different in the carnival. That's what excited her. They were different from anything she knew.

In the shower, with the shampoo suds running down her neck, she thought she smelled cotton candy. She'd taken Todd and Daisy again when the rides started up at two and, in the afternoon heat, the whole fairgrounds had smelled like hogs and caramel corn. There was a girl there no older than she was selling tickets in a booth and a baby, that had to be hers, lying asleep on the floor. It had startled Suelinda, seeing the baby there, with a pacifier in its mouth, and its hair damp on its neck.

Not that she didn't know girls her age who had babies. She knew girls who were sixteen and had babies just to get out on their own. But what it was that seemed hard to get a grasp of was to be *that* girl you'd have a baby, *and* you'd travel with the carnival. Suelinda couldn't fathom it. She couldn't make what that would be like come clear in her mind. She shut the shower off and toweled herself dry and took the hair dryer into her bedroom.

When she was dressed, when she'd finished with her hair, she went out and looked at herself sideways in the hall mirror. She had on her pink sandals and her best shorts and the pink top she'd bought on Saturday and she knew from the mirror just what kind of once-over she'd get from Joel when he saw her. She looked good. She looked terrific, in fact, and she went in and sat down on the bed and did her toenails in "Racy Plum," waiting, and went through a stack of movie magazines until the doorbell rang.

He was two minutes early. Boys were always early or on time until they were sure of you, and she put a Kleenex and four dollars in her shorts pocket and went downstairs to let him look at her. He seemed like a boy to her, standing at the door—the funny way he grinned at her without meeting her eyes. He seemed like a boy even more than Jerry did, and it came to her all at once how the man at the carnival had taken her in—totally—with just a flicker of his eyes and she wondered what in the world it was a man like that could do to you that a boy—even a boy like Jerry Henderson—had never even thought of.

"You ready for the skydive?"

"I am," Suelinda said, and they went down the front steps and waited for Todd to shoot by them on his Hot Wheel.

At the fairgrounds, all the rides were going, and Dolly Parton was blaring out on the loudspeaker at the radio booth.

"Wait a minute. I like this song," Suelinda said, pulling on Joel's arm, and she put her hands on her hips, listening.

"There you are. Miss Dolly Parton," the announcer said. "And you all know how she gets dressed. *In nothing flat!*"

Joel was laughing and Suelinda pushed her arm through his and hooked her finger in the belt loop of his jeans. "Oh, you men sure like a joke," she said, turning her eyes up at him. "I thought we were taking the skydive."

It was when they were at the top of it, ready for the car to plummet toward the earth, and she was hanging on to Joel and he had his arm tight around her, that she saw the girl from the ticket booth again. She was leaning on the door of a trailer and fanning herself with a towel.

"See that girl?" Suelinda asked, and then the car dropped and the air rushed up over her windpipe and she screamed.

"She was right there," she said afterward when they were walking past the booth with the toy pandas in it. She pointed toward the trailer.

"Who?" Joel said, and Suelinda waved at her Aunt Sue who was the bigger part of who she was named for and had on a painted felt hat with gold tassels hanging from it.

"Just this girl my age that was selling tickets before. She had a baby. Can you imagine that traveling with a carnival?"

Joel shrugged, and Suelinda kept her eyes on the trailer while she waited for him to get her a snow cone. The girl was inside there right this minute, she thought. Maybe she'd washed her baby in a plastic washtub and put it to bed. Maybe she was getting ready to go back to work. Maybe she was in there talking to who she was married to or whoever it was that baby's father was.

Suelinda took the snow cone and tilted it up and drank out of the side. Joel was shooting an air rifle now, trying to win her a stuffed dog, and she had one eye on him and the other on the trailer. Maybe that man was in there with the girl. Maybe he was an escaped convict himself who'd forced the girl to go in the carnival with him. Maybe he was a man with a wife somewhere he couldn't see because of a stake-out. Maybe that girl had just plain stolen him from another woman.

The last idea seemed like a fact, all at once, and a picture flashed into Suelinda's mind that was like a picture on TV or in the movies, of a girl stretched out naked on a bed with a man towering above her and another woman, with hard eyes appearing suddenly in the door-way and the girl grabbing at the sheets to pull them over her. Suelinda could see the whole thing, but where she was looking from was the bed and the woman in the doorway with the hard eyes was the girl with the baby.

"Well I won it for you. Where's my thank-you?" Joel said, and Suelinda took the dog from him and gave him a squeeze around the waist and kissed his cheek.

"I guess I get it later," he said into her ear, and Suelinda took his hand and started off for the crafts and flowers building.

"Come on," she said. "I got cousins that win blue ribbons, don't you? There's no living with them if you don't look."

Walking through the weaving display, she thought she talked to half the people in town: "I don't know if they set the court date yet." "Well, he's been real busy, Mr. Henry. It's his busy season at the store, so maybe that's why it's late. I'll tell him to call you when I get home." "They were pretty good, except Todd tried to get himself lost." "No, I had a postcard, but that's all."

Suelinda headed for the flowers, and Joel picked up a big bou-quet and stuck it on his head, fanning out the gladioli like feathers.

"Hey, set that down!" Eunice Price straightened up in the mid-dle of the tables all at once, her garden club tag glittering in the light and her finger wagging at them. "Joel Krieke and Suelinda Elly, I'm surprised at you."

"Sorry, Miss Price," Suelinda said and Joel tickled her in the back and she half choked to death to keep herself from laughing.

"I suppose you want to see all the chickens. You want to see every rabbit and little pig?" Joel said when they got outside, and Suelinda glanced at the trailer and shook her head.

"I don't care. We could go on the octopus. Did you see if they brought those animals they were talking about?"

"There're some birds down there. You can hear them," Joel said, and they started walking down the row of booths, past the man with the oiled chest who was playing the shell game and the beckoning woman with the bracelets all the way up both arms (Suelinda had already stared at her awhile and decided she was a washed-up belly dancer or a retired madam), past the floating ducks and glittering T-shirts, the canned screams booth and the three-minute charcoal portraits.

"Well is this it?" Suelinda asked, disappointed. They had stopped in front of the last booth, which was empty except for a pair of blue and gold parrots in a cage and a greenish-yellow canary.

"So who said they were having animals?"

"Animals? You want animals, sweetie?"

"It's that bird talking," Suelinda said, startled.

"You betcha, sweetie. Hey Pete, come on out. Hey Petie, we got you an audience."

Suelinda had her hands on Joel's arms, watching. There was a door at the back of the booth and it was opening now and a monkey scampered out with a cup in its hand. "Pay her. Pay her," the parrot screamed, and a boy next to them dropped a quarter in the cup.

"Folding money, buster," the parrot said, and Suelinda took out one of her dollar bills and waved it at the parrot and then put it in the cup. "What a looker! *Sweet*-heart," the parrot said, and Suelinda laughed and noticed there was a man standing in the doorway now, an old man in a felt hat and suspenders who was eating a sandwich.

"Slept through supper," he said. His voice had an odd, gravelly accent, and it seemed directed mostly at himself. "Princess!"

Suelinda looked back at the monkey.

"Princess is a dog!" the parrot howled.

"She is a dog," Suelinda said. She could just see a tiny gray poodle with earrings and a satin bow peeking out from behind the man's legs.

"Come on, Princess," the man said. He had finished his sandwich and he walked out and stood in the center of the floor with a hoop in his hand. "Princess," he said again, and the dog jumped through the hoop, which seemed about eight times her height, and Suelinda decided the old man looked grumpy but sweet, with lines in his face as deep as her great-grandfather had had when he died.

"Oh," she said, sucking her breath in.

"What?" Joel asked, and she shook her head. *The old man had numbers on his arm!* She had perfectly sharp eyes and she could seem them on his skin, a long row of numbers that started with a letter. That meant he'd been a prisoner. From somewhere she knew that meant he'd been a prisoner someplace.

Suelinda stared. So here was an old dog trainer, and even *he* must have been a prisoner—even someone like him! Maybe he'd been a safecracker when he was young. Maybe he still was. Maybe he was one of those people that lean up against the lock of a safe door, while they turn the knob, and listen to hear it click.

There was a small crowd gathered in front of the booth now, and the dog started to prance on its hind legs, and the monkey bowed in front of them with the cup.

"Joel, look at those numbers. There on his arm. See? He must've been in jail," she whispered.

Joel shook his head. "No," he said in her ear. "Maybe in Auschwitz. Maybe someplace like that," he said, but then the parrot was talking again.

"Pay her. Pay her, sweetie. Oh, what a looker! *Sweet*-heart."

"Let's go," Joel said, and Suelinda went after him through the crowd and nodded at her sister-in-law who was trying to look over the top of her head.

So leave it to Joel, she figured, to think he got something she didn't. Auschwitz what? If she knew anything, this old parrot man had killed somebody. She couldn't picture him with a gun in his hand, but she could see him with a knife. She could see him sneaking up on somebody with the blade glinting in the sun.

"You want good seats for that race, we better head for the grand-stand," Joel said.

"They're racing? I thought it was the demolition derby."

"Sure they're racing. They been practicing for it all week. The demolition part's for afterwards," Joel said, and he paid at the window.

When the cars were in the middle of their warm-up laps, Suelinda was thirsty. "Don't you think they'd have somebody selling Coke in the bleachers on a hot night like this?" she said, looking around. "Well I'll get us one. No, you sit there. I can do it."

She got up and she was halfway to the exit when she saw the man again. He was leaning against the railing about two feet from where she had to walk, and she thought he was looking straight at her.

"Oh, God," she said under her breath. Her stomach was balled up in a hard knot, and she turned her head to the side, pretending she was hunting for someone in the crowd, and she kept on walking, hop-ing she hadn't turned as pink all over as her clothes were. She could hear him breathing when she went by.

Outside the grandstand, she ran. It was as if some excitement had boiled up inside her and made her run. She ran all the way to the hot dog stand and then she forced herself to stand in line.

"Two Cokes—large," she told the vendor and for as much as the Coke sign seemed perched on the cook's head, what she was really looking at was in her mind, the man with the outsize belt buckle and the sheeny hair. She knew he'd eyed her with a look that was, for all the world, like a man in a movie who was burning up at the sight of a woman and straining to keep his hands off her.

Suelinda paid for the Cokes and picked them up and started slowly back across the fairgrounds. She couldn't think of what a man like that would talk about when he wasn't talking about pictures in the post office, just what he would say. She pried the cap of her cup up with her teeth and took a swallow. She had this scene in her mind. It was this dark night and it was still hot out and she was standing with the man behind the trailer and he had his arm straight-armed out to her shoulder and he was staring at her and she was waiting.

"Get out!" She could hear what he was saying all at once. She was reading his lips but she could hear him at the same time. He was spitting the words at her. "Get out. What is this, a setup? *Get!*"

Suelinda pushed the cap down on the Coke. Her hand had jerked a little to the side and some of the Coke had spilled down the cup. She could hear the man yelling at her exactly as though he were doing it, but what struck her even more, what she hadn't thought of until now, was what his hands would be like. She could see them moving in the darkness, all lit up like hands in a horror show, and they were bony, oddly elongated, and the nails were covered, as though they had to be, with grease.

Suelinda shook her head, trying to clear it. *I got too much of this heat*, she thought, and she licked at the dribble of Coke on the bottom of the cup. She was going to look at the man straight on. She was going to give him the same kind of stare he'd given her and see just exactly what it was he looked like. She put one of the Cokes on top of the other and held her hand up so the stamp showed for the ticket taker. She could hear the crowd yelling and the cars roaring around the track. Somewhere over to the left, Dolly Parton was singing again, but the song that was going through her own head, the song that was making her feel a little giddy and giggly was, "Just one look, da, da, da, da, THAT'S ALL IT TOOK! Yeah!" Suelinda pushed her shoulders back and started into the grandstand.

She was making her way around a knot of people when a shout went through the crowd. It seemed to come right up from the bleachers, rising over the noise of the cars, and then there was an enormous, collective gasp. Suelinda jumped and squeezed the Cokes so the top lid popped off. "What?" she said. The man was gone and everyone was standing up in front of her and there were screams all over the place and then, as if somebody had slammed a door shut, it was quiet.

"What happened?" Suelinda hurried up the steps to Joel. She squeezed in beside him.

"Eighty-four." Joel's eyes were fixed on the track, and she saw the car now. It was on fire just inside the infield and it was split nearly in two.

A siren had started up in the distance and the other cars were stopped at crazy angles on the track and people were running everywhere.

"So who's eighty-four?" she asked.

Joel craned at the program the man in front of them had. "LaVern Cobb. I never heard of him."

"He must be from away. They stopping the race then?"

"I guess they'll pull him out if they can."

A siren was screaming outside on the road and the fire truck roared onto the track and the firemen were scrambling around, working at the hoses and an ambulance pulled up behind them. Suelinda's eyes roved through the crowd. She couldn't see the man. She couldn't find him anywhere. "Here's your Coke," she said, remembering, and she drank hers and kept looking around.

"They're getting him out now." Joel was like he had his breath sucked away. "I wish I brought my binoculars."

"How come you'd want to look?" Suelinda put her cup down and crushed it with her foot. "You think they'll race any more?"

"It looks like his leg's half off."

Suelinda glanced down the row. She thought she'd spotted the girl with the baby and she kept watching out of the corner of her eyes, but when the person she was looking at turned around, it was somebody else. She scratched her leg. "You got any of your Coke left?"

"I don't think he even moved. Here."

The car was still smoking and the drivers from the other cars were out leaning on their cars, looking.

"Well it must be over, Joel," Suelinda said when the ambulance siren started again. "Look. The track's all ripped up there. Did he roll? What happened to the loudspeaker? They for sure won't race anymore tonight. We might as well leave."

"Did you see him? I think his face was charred. All right, we can go. But where to? It's not even nine thirty yet."

"The Ferris wheel's running." Suelinda pointed at the top arc of cars that was curving through the air behind the grandstand. "We didn't ride that yet. We could ride it and we never tried the octopus. I guess they won't give you your money back for this, but they should." Suelinda had Joel's hand and she kept searching through the crowd while they walked down to the exit.

In the night outside the grandstand, all the rides were lit up and moving like giant sparklers writing in the sky.

"It's pretty," Suelinda said, pushing the stuffed dog up higher under Joel's arm, "even if it is still hot. I think a carnival's pretty. Let's just walk around." She was looking at the booths, hunting through the people running the rides.

"What was his name again?" Joel asked.

"Who?"

"Eighty-four."

"LaVern Cobb—you said it was."

"I think he was dead."

"Well who'd want to race one of those cars anyway? It's dumb." Suelinda rattled the change in her pocket. They'd stopped walking and they were in the darkness only a little way off from the trailer where she'd seen the girl in the afternoon.

"I really do think he was dead."

"Well maybe he is." Suelinda could see the curtain in the trailer moving faintly in the air. "Look at that trailer. It's got stickers from all over. There's Florida and California. What's that bottom one? Is it Texas?"

Suelinda closed her eyes, listening to the sounds around her— the music from the merry-go-round and the long wail of a cow from the animal barns. She was seeing something different in her mind now—some Texas night and a shoot-out and drugs—she thought there'd be drugs—and the old safecracker, turned in by the madam, dying with a contorted grin on his face in a hail of bullets and the carnival man escaping somehow—paying for his freedom by forcing the girl on another man.

Suelinda felt a shiver along her spine.

"Can you feel what it's like here, Joel?" she said, opening her eyes and curling herself into his shoulder. She bit the tip of his earlobe and ran her tongue behind his ear.

"They're all dangerous, dangerous people," she said. She held on to his wrists and stared hard into his eyes. She could feel the blood surging up to her temples and her heart racing. "I *love* it, Joel," she said, whispering against his shirt collar. "I'm scared to death."

Hubbub, Indigo, Castle of Rain

There was a rattle, a hiss and vibrant thumping in the radiator next to the wall and Manon Josten, the girl in the front corner desk, looked up from her math paper and rubbed the eraser of her pencil along her nose. All afternoon the fourth grade had smelled like pizza from hot lunch, but now that the radiator had started up, there was a stale, scorched odor to the air that was like the smell of cotton burning.

Manon sniffed. Radiators were as new to her as her classmates were, and she wondered if there was something wrong with this one. But no one else in the room seemed to have noticed—half of the class was still bent over multiplication problems, and the other half was reading with the teacher—and she decided the radiator was all right. She sniffed again. The pizza smell had disappeared, and she was glad it had. Since noon she had been thinking off and on of asking her mother to let her buy lunch, and every time she thought of it, she felt cross. She knew the answer. Other mothers warned their children about interesting things—about Satan or godless baby killers—but her mother thought white bread and bologna were the real dangers in life. Manon did not think her mother even understood the temptation to eat something that was nonorganic or refined, something that had been heated in cellophane.

She got up and went to the pencil sharpener. She felt tall walking. She was a tall girl particularly in the legs and, as she held her pencil in the sharpener and looked down, she had the sudden thought that her feet looked farther away than they had even last week and that idea made her cross, too. She was in no hurry to grow up. *That* was one of the things in her life she was definite about.

"No, Tim. Luh-MONT, not LAY-mont," Mrs. Thorson said, and Manon leaned her face against the window frame and looked outside. Only a part of the school yard was visible from the window. The lower wing of the building, which jutted out under a gnarl of clouds, cut the playground in two, but from her vantage point, she could see that the usual ripple of grass in the far outfield of the baseball diamond and the hard pack of dirt under the jungle gym had turned into huge puddles of muddy water. Where the right end of the swing sets rose against the sky, the whole world looked the color of galvanized steel.

It was not raining now. The first rain had come at nine o'clock with an enormous crack of thunder that sent shrieks through the classroom. All day long the rain had fallen and stopped and then started again, sometimes gushing in a steady downpour, sometimes blowing hard against the windows. But for the last hour, the sky had been sullen and quiet.

Manon leaned closer to the window. She saw something now she had not seen before. Outside, where the long row of bricks that divided one window from another protruded at right angles, there was an immense, silvered spider's web. It had caught the rain. In each dimension it held light-filled drops of water that made a dazzle of intricate, transparent shapes.

She wedged her face tighter against the windowpane, looking. Try as she could, she could not see the spider that had made the web but, as she pressed her face against the glass, she felt a quick stab in her ribs and, jumping, she crushed a paper airplane underfoot. In some haste, she went back to her desk.

"Who knows what a 'hubbub' is?" Mrs. Thorson was looking for hands in the reading class. "A babble of voices? All right."

Manon made a quick charge down the last row of her math problems and turned her eyes back over the page. She knew what a hubbub was then. It was the commotion in foreign cities where people spoke a language you couldn't understand. And it was the noise on the bus after school when the high school students were riding and said all the words you didn't really want to hear.

She turned her math page over and looked back out the window. She did not have *that* to go through today anyway. In the morning, her mother had promised to pick her up at four. The idea was that she'd have a chance after school to play with the girls who walked home. Now with the rain, there wasn't much hope anyone would stay on the playground, but half of Manon's intention was intact anyway. She had not told her mother the rest, that she hated riding the bus with the high school students. She detested it, and this afternoon she wouldn't have to.

She put her head down on her arms and closed her eyes and then squinted them open back and forth, watching the shadow her hand threw shift on the desk. The room was starting to feel warm. She could hear the giggle and shuffle of the kindergartners out in the hall on their way to the bathrooms. She sniffed. The burning smell had disappeared. What she smelled now was bubble gum. She lifted her head, but no one was chewing anything. Nobody's cheek looked puffy.

Mrs. Thorson put her reading book on her desk and caught a pencil that almost fell off. She tugged on the state map so that it rolled away with a loud rush. "Math group, hand your papers up," she said. "There's enough time for spelling."

A flutter of papers came over Manon's shoulder. She put her own paper on top and then straightened the stack and passed it across the aisle. Behind her, someone was squeaking a shoe heel against the floor and on the other side of the room books were slamming shut, but Manon was all attention. When it was spelling time, she was always called on first.

"Indigo," Mrs. Thorson said, pointing at her with a piece of chalk. Outside the wind picked up and the loose gutter at the corner of the building smacked against the bricks.

"Indigo. I-n-d . . ." Manon felt her heart race. "E. No, i." She had seen Mrs. Thorson's face tighten. "G-o."

"I-n-d-i-g-o," Mrs. Thorson said, writing on the blackboard, and Manon relaxed in her desk. *Indigo. Indigo, indigo.* She liked the word. It reminded her of calico. The two words sounded alike to her and together they made her think of country things, of this school, this place. But indigo sounded dark, too, mysterious somehow, and that really intrigued her.

The windows were shaking in their frames, and Manon flattened her palms against the desk, glad that it felt solid. This was the first time she had gone to a school with so many and such big windows. She wondered if all country schools were like this—tall ceilings and round, milky light fixtures and wooden desks with creases in the top for holding pencils, and floors that groaned and buckled in front of the library shelves—if every child who rode the school bus home had hair that smelled, at times, a little of sweat, a little like somebody's cow barn.

"Charm-ing," Mrs. Thorson said, and Manon listened to the boy at the end of the row spell out the letters and counted them on her fingers as he said them. She thought of the schools she'd been to. Including the year of infant school in London, it was six schools now.

"Perfect. This is perfect! I've always wanted to live in the country," her mother had said when they saw the school the first day, but Manon had felt her mother was mentally somewhere else—at home in the new house maybe, sizing up the kitchen for wallpaper, her gold chain bracelet glittering on her wrist, or standing in front of her closet deciding what she would wear when Manon's new stepfather got home from his business trip to Chicago and New York. Manon had watched her mother walk down the aisle between the classroom desks, smoothing the wood under her fingers, and then she had gone ahead herself and explained to Mrs. Thorson how to pronounce her name—that it started like "manna" and ended with the sound like the "o-n" in song. She waited while Mrs. Thorson practiced saying it, and she looked at how gray Mrs. Thorson's hair was.

Manon had liked the school all right, but she liked the house even better and its basket of vegetables her mother kept full by the back door and the smell of the herbs that hung over the sink. And she thought she liked her stepfather, though it was odd to smell the scent of his skin on the pillows of her mother's bed, hard to call him Joe, totally impossible to say Dad. Most of all, she liked riding the bus in the morning when there weren't any high school students. She was the first one to get on and the bus carried her away, rolling downhill into patches of ground fog, flying straight past fields of cornstalks that had turned the color of pampas grass and plums.

"That's enough for today." Mrs. Thorson dotted the "i" on "chipmunk" and put her chalk down on the ledge of the blackboard. "First row, dismissal," she said as the bell rang, and there was an instant, busy traffic to the cloakroom.

Today, since she didn't have to hurry to find a seat on the bus, Manon did not mind that her row was the last to be called. She walked slowly out of the room. By the time she'd put her sweater on and hoisted her backpack onto her shoulder, most of the class had disappeared. Some people were ready for rain. There was a great tromping of boots in the halls, like an army marching through, and there were plastic slickers and fisherman's hats in bright colors bobbing out the doors.

Manon took her time walking down the hall. She could see the buses out front. They were lined up along the curb and, as hers pulled away, it seemed to her to rock from the noise inside. She buttoned her sweater. Maybe there was someone left on the playground, someone to spy on from a corner while she waited for her mother. She went outside and walked to the end of the building, the wind pushing her along.

But who would stop to play on a field that was rutted with mud or on canvas swings filled with water? Except for a handful of children waiting at the crosswalk at the far end of the playground, there was no one to see. Manon looked toward the parking lot, half hoping that her mother had come early to get her, but their car wasn't there. A last straggler from one of the lower grades had run out of the building and got in the cab of a pickup truck, and his mother drove away now but her mother was nowhere in sight.

Manon pulled her collar up and pressed her back against the side of the building. The wind had given her gooseflesh, but it was bumping the clouds across the sky and, toward the west in the direction the bus went, the far hills were topped with a widening strip of deep and purplish blue. Her mother would be in no hurry to get her, she decided. She would not think about the rain. At home the sky would already have cleared and all she would see was sunshine.

A piece of cement was cracked and loosened in the sidewalk, and Manon nudged her foot under it and pushed. She thought of the bus stuttering along its route, stopping at crossroads and farmhouses, the noise inside exploding through the door as it crooked open. She was definitely not sorry to be here. If she walked, if she jogged a little, she would not even be cold. And if she followed the sidewalk around the building, keeping under the overhang, she would stay dry and have a chance for a closer look at the spider's web. The idea presented itself to her all in a piece, and she was instantly persuaded.

She went around the building. The first room was the third grade room and the lights were off but Manon, peering through the window, could still see the huge apple drawn on the blackboard. She edged along the bricks to the next room—her room—and saw Mrs. Thorson at the desk writing in her grade book. Manon watched for a moment. Then she counted windows down the row to the one by the pencil sharpener and looked for the spider's web. It was just as she had seen it, a castle with rooms of sheerest filament and furnished with rain, but it was larger now and there was a hard and shiny spider at its center, its legs moving like treadles.

Manon stopped perfectly still. She had seen spiders spin their webs before but she had never imagined a web so intricate or so large. She touched her throat and watched, her breath caught in her chest.

The spider's legs were paddling through the air. They were moving, and Manon's eyes followed, shuttling, as if threaded, up and down. The web grew. The light went off in the classroom and she could almost hear Mrs. Thorson's footsteps on the floor and the door closing, and still she watched. She could not have said how long she stood there, nor could she have said when it was she knew she was not alone. She had heard nothing but the wind. There had been no abrupt movement in the shadows that fell across her feet, across the spider's web. Still there was something. The skin between her shoulders felt open, prickly.

Manon drew her shoulder blades in, her eyes fixed on the spider's legs. It was as if the converging sight lines of someone else's eyes had settled on her back. Carefully she looked up. She looked to the top of the highest pane, sorting through the reflections in the glass. There were clouds moving; the tops of trees shivered in the wind. Manon lowered her eyes down the murky darkness of the glass. At first she could not see anything, but slowly—compressing gradually into focus—she saw the wavy image of a man.

He was coming closer. Manon did not think she knew him. He was wearing a plaid shirt, but he wasn't the janitor, and he didn't say her name. Yet they were together in this mirror, she in the front and he in the back beyond her shoulder, and she wondered if the glass made him farther away than he really was. He had stopped walking. He was looking at her in the glass, and then Manon saw him unzipping himself, saw him fumbling at himself, moving his hand.

She stood as if grown to the spot. *A babble of voices.* There were voices in her head, the words on the bus, but she couldn't hear them. There was too much din, too much static, like a chorus of crickets in her ears. She stood, her eyes frozen still in the glass.

Then—a scent in the air, a sweetish, scarred odor—the man had stopped, had backed away and, in the window, Manon saw only leaves and the sky.

She did not turn her head at once. When she did turn, her eyes followed the horizon as she had watched the spider's path. Beyond the playground, the man was running against violet clouds, his body a dark cutout fleeing across the gray sun.

Manon closed her eyes. Still she could see him. But when she opened her eyes, he was gone.

She shifted her feet. She picked up first one and then the other, slowly, as if she were lifting the weight of the ground. She turned her head to one side and then hunched her hands into her pockets and started walking along the building. When she reached the corner and saw the parking lot, she was nearly running. Still her mother hadn't come.

Manon blinked. She was cold—her teeth were chattering. But her mother *was* coming now. Their Fiat was slowing to turn onto the school road. Manon felt her backpack and hurried off across the playground.

"Oh, babe—goodness you're frozen." Her mother pushed the car door open. There was a surge of warm air from the heater through the door, and when her mother hugged her, Manon smelled perfume and heat. Her mother's eyes crinkled, smiling. "You're blue!"

Manon put her backpack on the floor. Her teeth were chattering hard and she pulled her knees up to her chest.

"You'll be warm in a minute." Her mother hugged her again. She put the car in reverse. "Oh, this mud! It's like the monsoon hit. Joe's home. He got back at noon."

Manon darted a look at her mother and then turned back and stared at the cornfield on the side of the road.

"So tell me what you did today."

Manon kept studying the field, memorizing the purple in the husks. "Not that much," she managed between chatters.

"You must have learned something." Her mother looked at her expectantly, her earrings dangling just below the scarf she had tied on. It was Manon's favorite, of fringed cotton with silk-screened butterflies. Her mother was pretty, she knew. She looked healthy, like the foods she ate.

"I don't know," Manon said.

"There must have been something." Her mother laughed a throaty, warm laugh, swinging the car in a tight curve onto the highway, and Manon wanted to bury her head there on her mother's neck where her curls were loose below the scarf, to hide in the moist scent of her mother's skin, in the fragrant shifting of the butterflies. She wanted to show her mother the spun-out thread of the spider's web, to tell her, to say, if she had to, the words on the bus . . .

Manon turned and looked through the window. "I learned what a 'hubbub' is," she started. She glanced swiftly back at her mother and she was thinking with the whole pressure of her mind of what she meant to say. The words were pushing, hurting her tongue. She leaned forward, watching her mother as she watched the road.

But there was some forbidding roundness in the way her mother's hands gripped the steering wheel, something impassable that closed down hard in front of the words, an aura about her mother of places she was going or had been. A lush scent of knowing. Some rough, stirring breath of Manon's own future.

Manon looked down at her feet. She moved a little and then leaned her head against the window. She pulled at her lip.

"And I learned to spell indigo," she said. The words fell softly, placed in the air. She closed her eyes. She pushed her knees down and let her feet rest on top of her backpack.

"Indigo," she said. She raised her voice. "Indigo. I-n, d-i, g-o."

Turkey Run

John Mettlie's wife, Rennie, started down the stairs, feeling her way along the railing in the dark. She could still hear the jangle of the alarm clock going through her.

Two o'clock in the morning. Rennie reached with her toes for the last step. She felt the door to the living room at her shoulder and pushed. The ridge of the floorboards rose under her feet. She nudged the door shut behind her and fumbled for the light switch. The room went gray. Rennie, her eyes aching and blinking in the light, counted last summer's moths in the ceiling fixture and told herself it needed cleaning.

"But not now," she said, heading for the kitchen. The house was cold, and she leaned down to open the wood stove. There were still embers. She blew on them, her lips pursed and steady. Finally a flame spurted upward into the dark vault of the stove, and she crossed the ashes with kindling and closed the door.

The house was totally quiet. Rennie stood looking at the floor. It seemed she had been alone for days. Upstairs her husband was sick, still burning sick with the flu, and all week long there had been only one visitor, a plump girl missionary holding a toddler in her arms and talking about the Lord, about a messenger of the Lord, a conflagration of piety glowing in her eyes.

There was a crackling noise in the stove, and Rennie put a log in slantwise across the kindling. Seeing the girl and child at the door had reminded her of when her own children were young, and so did getting up alone at night this way. There had been two bedrooms for three babies and she, groggy and barely out of her teens, had stood stock still in the hallway in the middle of the night, collecting herself, thinking which room it was that the crying came from. And now her daughter was married and in Milwaukee in her own bedroom in her own trailer, one son had gone to the army and the other was trapping in Canada, and Rennie was by herself in the night again with something she had to do.

She pushed another log onto the fire. Before bed she had laid out all her clothes but now in the cold, with the light from the living room flaring in at the doorway and the kitchen windows bare, she had a sudden bout of modesty. She took her bathrobe off and pulled her clothes on quickly over her nightgown—a T-shirt, a sweater, and jeans—and stuffed her underwear in the pockets of her robe. Her work boots were standing with the men's next to the stove and she sat down and tugged them on. Shit-kickers, her sons called them, and she had railed against the name forever, sometimes at the top of her lungs, but quietly, secretly, irrevocably, she had started to say the word herself.

"Tied shit-kickers," she said, stretching her feet out in front of her.

Rennie looked at the clock. In twelve minutes, the first truck was due. She would hear its horn blaring up from the road and she would wave her flashlight, its beam carrying from the top of the driveway, southward, down, and the truck would shift, its brakes sputtering and coughing, and send up an unearthly roar as it climbed the driveway to her.

Rennie glanced at the ceiling, one brief look in the direction of John Mettlie sleeping in bed. Then she stood up and drank a glass of water at the sink. She had to hurry. She was hurrying now. She pulled her jacket and hat on and saw herself dimly in the window glass, and she did not look so very different from the girl who twenty years ago, though out of reach of the voters (determined as she was to marry her brother's friend, John Mettlie—wonderfully, irresistibly older), was voted best looking in school. Rennie pushed her hair up under her stocking cap and, taking a flashlight from the shelf, opened the door.

It was cold out but it was still not cold enough. Rennie slogged through the mud in the yard. She did not remember when it had ever stayed above freezing into December and rained. Rained, rained, rained. There had been so much rain that it seemed, at times, the whole world was no longer in a solid state. Even now with a snatch of stars visible in the sky, there were drops of rain spitting at her in the wind.

The dogs came out of the barn, their heads slung low on their chests. Rennie collared the younger one and tied it up. "Crow," she said, and the other dog, the older dog, followed after her.

Rennie switched her flashlight on. The fence that swayed out from the corners of the barn stretched ahead, ascending the pasture in converging lines. She dipped her flashlight over the barnyard. Cattle were scattered and sleeping, the remnant of the herd; the piebald horse her children had ridden summers ago, and abandoned to a lazy old age of long hooves and a blowsy mane that surrounded his shoulders like a cape, was standing at the fence.

"Hello, Pie," she said, using the old fond nickname, and the horse opened one dark eye and pushed his nose into her sleeve.

Rennie hunted in the sky. The stars were gone, and except for the backlit opening of gray where the moon had been, all the sky was as black as the cattle. She climbed the fence beyond the barn. She could hear rain blowing down in the far trees and, a moment later, felt it splashing cold against her knuckles. Ahead, where the fence curved west, Crow slid under the gate and disappeared. Rennie hurried, fighting the ground, her face turned into her shoulder, away from the rain. The west gate was shut. It was latched in two places. She looked out across the fence to where the turkeys slept, ranged like masses of pillows against the hillsides.

"Crow," she called, an image floating in her mind of their first run of turkeys two months ago when a prowler had opened the gates in the night and the cows had descended on the turkeys when the truck was loading. The night sky had exploded with bellowing and feathers and John had threatened to sell the whole rest of the herd in the morning or to forget this turkey venture that was meant to replace cattle since the boys were grown and in another year, the two of them—John and Rennie Mettlie—would be alone.

Rennie heard the truck. She could see the north gate was closed, secure, and she was trying to run and thought in a flash she should have ridden the horse to check the gates and be charging down the driveway now to meet the truck, her legs dangling an inch above the ground and Pie dressed primly, Lady Godiva–like, in his hair. A siege of laughter welled up in her as she rounded the barn.

It stayed with her in waves that she fought back as the truck shuddered up the drive, and it squirted out in little jets of burbled noise when Crow raced up to her but finally, with the ground trembling beneath her feet and a semi truck idling violently in front of her, she was calm.

"Where do we load?" The driver in the truck looked down at Rennie and then beyond her as if hunting for the men he meant to talk to.

Rennie stiffened. "John's sick. The boys aren't here. You can pull in over there."

"Yes ma'am." The driver drawled his answer out. He was maybe fifty with a face that looked planed to make it lie flat and, as she looked at him and the picture of herself on horseback came back to her, Rennie felt the urge to laugh rushing over her again. She turned away. The ground rumbled hard under her and the truck crawled up the driveway, the exhaust from its stack smoking in the rain.

"We're shorthanded," the driver said, climbing out of the cab. "They're loading early down on the county road. You don't have any men to help?"

"No." Rennie felt the lint in the seam of her pocket. "I need somebody to help bring the turkeys down. That's all. I've got the dog, and there's snow fence up the whole way."

The driver looked at her and then off toward the road at the sound of another truck. "There's the loader now." He snagged Rennie's wrist as she started forward with the flashlight. "I set a flare. You don't have to go."

Rennie pulled her hand back. "Fine," she said, her voice hissing in the rain, but there was the sound of a door opening in the cab behind them and, to Rennie's surprise, another man was getting out. He was younger than the driver. He was not far from her own age, she guessed, and sleek with an iron face like a Marlboro cowboy's, and he looked unmarried, or, as her mother would say, not much married.

Rennie felt a warm spot at the base of her neck, and she backed off the gravel, her boots sagging into the ground as the loader truck pulled up behind the semi. Her own marriage, she thought, showed all over her. It was impossible to hide.

"Pete, go on up with her and start the birds while we get the loader set," the driver said. There were four men now, counting the ones from the loader, and Rennie turned off up the field, whistling softly to Crow, not waiting to see who Pete was.

She heard him walking behind her. The rain had long since started to soak into her jeans and her stocking cap. She pulled her hood up from inside her jacket and fastened it at her chin. The man was still following behind her, navigating the mud of the field at the same trudging pace. She did not turn around. Her face stung. Her eyes itched from the rain. Water dripped down her nose and from the corners of her mouth. Behind her, she heard the scratching sound of a match striking a matchbox. She smelled a pinch of sulfur, imagined a thin burst of smoke.

Rennie turned the flashlight off and pushed the glass end into her pocket. They had gone through the gate to the first turkey shelter, and she picked up two of the wooden stakes that were leaning against its side.

"Here," she said, turning around to the Marlboro man. She felt a little unsteady, still ready to laugh. Even before the cigarette, she had known it was him.

He took the stake she offered without looking at her, his eyes turned across the turkey range.

"We can start over there." She pointed with her own stake to a splotch of white curved against the hill and, when he nodded, she began walking again, half thinking that in five months of raising turkeys she'd never known one to use a shelter in the rain and thinking harder that this man's face, in the dark, seemed impenetrable, a lacquered bronze that would barely change from winter to fall.

They had come to the first cluster of turkeys. Crow had gone ahead and, as Rennie climbed the range, she heard the turkeys moving in his wake, a ripple of sound that rolled and rolled away. She was walking straight into the rain now, the turkeys a dim, expanding stretch of light that pulsed before her. She stumbled. There was a flutter of wings. A turkey hunched into her face, its black eye glittering in a ring of peach flesh. Rennie caught herself. She'd gone down on one knee in the mud, and she pushed off the other knee and stood up. The turkeys were squealing around her. Up close the sound was thicker, a kind of barking, but from the edge of the light, it pushed toward her like the floating cry of flying birds. The sound came shrilly in layers, a kind of churchlike, fugal noise.

"Beyond that hill," Rennie said, clearing her throat—"we can start them down from there."

They had passed the far side of one batch of turkeys and were skirting the next. The man was walking even with her now. His lantern swayed between them, and Rennie could see the turkey feathers that were scattered across the range. Twice, from the corner of her eye, she thought they were snow.

"There?" the man asked, pointing with his stake, and Rennie nearly jumped. She had gotten used to the sound of him, the stubborn slapping of his boots against the mud and the rustle of his jacket, but his voice had surprised her.

She nodded. "You take the corner. I'll start them. We'll close toward the fence." She waited, but the man headed into the flock and grabbed a turkey by the legs. He held it screeching in the air.

"Weight's OK. All right, you can go."

Rennie stared at him, amazed. She felt a sudden surge of anger. He was judging the kind of turkey farmers they were. He was judging her.

She spun on her heel in the mud and went up the range. The ground was higher there, and had drained better. It was firmer under foot, and she stomped over it with her boots, glad to be by herself again. The man had unsettled her. She was not sure how, but it had been something more than his effrontery with the turkey.

"Crow," Rennie called. She was starting the turkeys now, prodding them. They were like cattle, docile and stubborn all at once, and Rennie herded them the way she herded cattle, slow and easy, her arms flapping, her right arm extended by the full length of the stake. She had turned the flashlight back on and held it in her left hand and, as her arm moved, the light went up and down, dissolving stripes across the sky and on the turkeys. They were moving, some of them flustered, gobbling awake. In the light their heads were pink and lavender, and they bobbed smoothly forward like swimmers doing the breaststroke.

Crow had come up and was working the far edge of the flock now, driving the strays in. He circled around them, diving at their feet, pushing them back into the flock, back into a flurrying huff of wings.

"Easy, easy. They're turkeys, not cows." Rennie shone the flashlight on Crow, and he looked around at her and then went back to work. His fur was stringy from the rain.

They were moving downhill now, the turkeys pressing up against each other, their squeals growing sharper. Rennie felt the ground go pulpy again beneath her boots. The rain had soaked under her jacket sleeves halfway up her arms. She couldn't see the man. He was holding the corner, though, forcing the turkeys along the fence. She could tell from the bulge of turkeys beside her. They were climbing on each other's backs. In front of her a turkey was down in the mud, his body twitching while the others walked over him. Rennie shoved the flashlight into her pocket and pushed a way clear with the stake and pulled the turkey upright. It was covered with mud and she scraped at it with her fingernails, but the turkey spurted away, lunging on with the flock, one muddy wing hanging broken at its side.

There were other turkeys down. Rennie tripped on a turkey that was drowned in a puddle and felt water squishing in over her boot top. There were turkeys sliding in the mud and moving sideways and backward and scrunching up together.

"They're backed up! They're closing too fast!" She was yelling as loud as she could, but she had no idea if the man had heard her. Then she saw him ahead, cutting the turkeys deftly out of the flock and circling them back, pulling turkey after turkey free of the mud. The line was narrowing. He was feeding turkeys toward the gate.

Rennie hesitated, watching. He had salvaged the thing by himself. She would give him that.

"Take the gate," he called, spotting her.

Rennie slipped, her feet shooting out in front of her, and sat down hard in the mud. "Take it yourself!" She was screaming, but silently, the way she'd taught her children to scream when they were small, with her neck pumping the noise instead of her lungs, lips mouthing the words. Rennie dragged herself out of the mud and picked up her stake.

He had not laughed anyway. Rennie's throat was burning, and she went on down the hill, her face turned away from the man, and she stationed herself beyond the gate. The turkeys were marching through, the bumps on their noses riding the air. Ahead, Rennie could see the trucks with their headlights shining through the rain. There was plywood up to make a pen, and the loader was in place, rising like a gangplank to the wall of cages on the semi. She aimed the turkeys toward the pen, and they kept going, obedient, heading straight, as John would say, for somebody's Christmas dinner. Rennie added up weights and dollars in her head.

"Take them on in," the driver said, heading past her up the range, and Rennie followed the first wave of turkeys into the pen. The loader belt was already running and the man, Pete, was standing on the platform in front of a cage. His eyes were moving over the turkeys. Then they settled on her. He motioned with his head, and Rennie made her way toward him through the turkeys. He reached a hand down over the belt and pulled her up beside him on the platform.

"Keep them headed straight. I'll work the cage doors," he said, and Rennie looked out at the whole sea of turkeys in front of her. Off beyond the plywood the driver was holding the flank in tight with Crow helping, and below her the other two men were catching turkeys, pushing them onto the loader belt. The whole flock had grown quieter and the turkeys riding the belt, gawking toward her, were absolutely still.

Rennie felt the platform rise. She was dizzy all at once, the loader vibrating under her feet. She pushed her fingers against her temples.

"You all right?" the man asked beside her.

Rennie nodded and started pushing turkeys sideways in the cage. She *was* all right. It was the belt that had gotten to her—the steady onslaught of it, the mechanical, jarring rhythm as it slid through the rain. She felt the wet feathers of turkeys, their solid bodies beating under her hands.

"Plant your feet. It's like an elevator." The man had reached over and pulled the cage door shut, and Rennie felt the loader jerking and sinking down to the next cage. She thought the man meant to steady her. His hands were almost at her shoulder, but he was opening the cage, waiting for her to lean out of the way. Rennie felt the warm spot come back on her neck. She squeezed a turkey too hard and it squawked in her ear.

She was warm all over when the first row of cages was filled. The man had gotten off the loader, and, even with the rain, Rennie was ready to take her jacket off and leave it on the cab seat where he was putting his, but she felt her nightgown rubbing under her jeans and she remembered her underwear stuck in the pockets of her bathrobe in the kitchen and she stopped unzipping her jacket at the throat.

He was back on the loader. Rennie could hear the rain pounding on the cab of the truck, feel it streaming from her face. She was getting used to this, to the pace that he kept, to what he needed her to do, to the steady, wet push of turkeys, the wrenching of cage doors, the hands jutting in and out of her vision, the arms crossing in front of her. She could hear the man breathe and she could smell tobacco on his breath and, on his skin when he leaned closer, that scent not quite of sweat but exertion, strength. She had known it all her life—this scent, this odor of maleness—first with her chin buried in her father's whiskers, riding in his arms, and later working as the need came, with brothers and uncles, husband, sons. But not like this. She had not known it before with a stranger.

Rennie blinked the rain out of her eyes and steered a turkey that was ready to fly off the belt, up into the cage. She was getting sleepy as well as warm. She started to yawn but wound up sneezing.

"You allergic to turkeys?" The man was pulling a cage door shut as he looked over his shoulder at her.

Rennie nodded, looking back at him, at the carved, perfect face, the hint of a smile. Then she shook her head quickly and laughed, embarrassed. "No, of course not," she told him.

The loader was moving. Rennie had her sea legs. For a second as it climbed, she thought she saw a light on upstairs in the house, that John was up, that he was making his way, feverish, along the wall to the bathroom, the light just touching the thinning strands of his hair. But the loader stopped and there was nothing, only darkness stretching away from the trucks. Rennie heard the cattle stirring in the barnyard.

"The noise makes them restless," she said.

"The night and the noise," the man answered, dark at her shoulder, and Rennie Mettlie, her ears throbbing with the noise of motors, of turkeys, of cattle and rain, thought with a sudden, dull unhappiness, of how it pleased her to be standing next to him.

When they were finished, when the last turkey was closed in the last cage and the whole truck seemed to burn with gleaming eyes, Rennie did not think she could talk. The rain had settled into a hard drizzle and it dripped off her nose while she huddled with the driver, signing papers. Behind her, she heard the sound of a match and the door of the truck slamming shut. She smelled sulfur again. She looked back at the solitary glow of a cigarette in the cab.

The driver gave her the carbons. "See you in March."

"Yes." Her voice was almost right. Rennie brushed the rain off her face and backed away from the trucks. She wanted to wait, but there was nothing to wait for.

"Crow," she called. He came wagging his tail, and Rennie ran her fingers along his wet fur. "Good job. I'll tell John. Good boy," she said. She started for the house. In her mind's eye she could see the turkeys losing their footing, one massive, truck-wide lurching forward as the truck began to move, but she didn't turn around. Headlights searched past her, the ground shook, and Rennie Mettlie kept walking. She could hear Basha, the younger dog, whining and starting to bark. When she reached the porch, she scratched his head, quieting him in the din of rain that rushed through the gutters.

"All right, Basha," she said when the trucks were gone. She untied him and watched as he shook himself and started after Crow.

Rennie opened the porch door and went inside. The kitchen was hot. A flicker of light from the stove threw a shadow on the wall behind the stack, and Rennie watched the flame move, the light from the living room shining dimly on her boots.

"Shit-kickers," she said. She walked across the room. "Shit-kickers," she said again, and she closed the damper on the stove and stood in front of the table, the rain from her jacket dripping on the floor. A puddle was forming at her feet, and water trickled across the floorboards. Rennie unzipped her jacket and hung it on a chair knob. She held her arms out over the stove and smelled the wool of her sweater heating up.

Shit-kickers. Shit-kickers and piebald. The two words were jostling each other in her head. And what was it the girl at the door had said, the baby nuzzling at her sleeve? *The Lord will bring you a messenger.* Rennie sat down. She could feel the laughter coming suddenly over her again, overpowering her, a hysteria engulfing her like the thunder of flying hoofbeats.

She held the edge of the table. The laughter twisted wildly inside her, stabbing her ribs, shattering inside her like glass.

Rennie held on.

Finally, spent, the sound stuttered away. Rennie stared at the table. She leaned back in the chair and rubbed her hand across her neck. She touched her cheek. She tried clearing her throat.

But it was simple enough. She could not get the smell of this man—the way that he moved—out of her mind.

Soundlessly, she eased her chair back to the floor. She lifted herself up from the table. She pulled her clothes off down to her nightgown and felt it wet at her ankles and wrists. She swayed a little on her feet.

"Go to bed, Rennie," she whispered, hugging her bathrobe into her cheek. She pushed herself forward, out of the room. The cat was sleeping on the sofa and the moths covered half the ceiling light. Rennie tiptoed upstairs.

"John?" There was no sound from the bedroom. She crept in the door and passed the dark, hunched rise of his shape in the bed. She felt her way to the dresser. Carefully she pulled a drawer open. The room smelled stale, of medicine and sickness. Rennie took her nightgown off and squirmed into a dry one that had shrunk in the wash.

"John?" She could hear him breathing as she got into bed. She folded her hands on the bedspread and stared up at the black expanse of the ceiling. She was seeing turkeys, turkeys and turkeys stretching through a whole night, and John Mettlie's breathing had finally lost its ragged edge.

"John," she said again, leaning on her side and whispering close to his ear. She waited, listening.

Rennie rolled back over. He did not hear her. He was deaf with sleep, and she listened to the rain tick against the shingles and slip down the roof in the darkness.

Violin Song

It was Gabe Jones's fate that the women in his life were music lovers. His wife, Lissy, was, and his mother and grandmother: Sonia Lindholm Jones, star singer in the Lutheran choir, and Francesca Caratini Lindholm—war bride from Salerno who, Italian or not, fixed *lefse* and made sausage like anybody's grandmother—Francesca, singer for the Catholics. What the three of them cared about wasn't rock or country or anything easy, but *real* music as his mother called it, and all Gabe's life somebody had looked at him eagerly when the music started, waiting for him to understand.

He didn't, and that fact was on his mind—stuck there—on a day he was under a car, working his fingers through grease to pull out a driveshaft. When he put his wrench in his pocket and rolled out from under the car, he was still as sure he'd never understand as he was unsure why he was quitting work in the middle of the day to take Lissy on the overnight trip she'd been wanting. More than that, he didn't get why this trip seemed to fall into the same category as musical expectations: things that made him uneasy.

However, it did. Gabe wiped the grease off his hands and hung the towel back on the garage wall. "Lock up when you leave, Tim," he said. He went over the plans in his mind—that Lissy had it arranged for the number to ring at Tim's if there was an accident, an emergency, that, besides Tim, Jake was on call for the night, that both Tim and Jake were working tomorrow until he and Lissy got back. She had the girls parceled out to the neighbors and she'd promised they'd be home by six.

Gabe hit the "no sale" button on the cash register and took the twenties and the checks out. He felt like a doctor, doing his last chassis and finishing at noon on a Wednesday. But Lissy had her heart set on their going away in the middle of the week. It was something different, she kept saying, and though Gabe was reluctant, the eagerness, the anxiousness in her voice had finally made him say yes. She had a bed and breakfast place reserved and she'd made a new dress. Gabe had even agreed to wear a suit for dinner, though he'd drawn the line at a flowered tie they saw in the Cities and Lissy had said OK when she looked at the price.

Gabe put his shirt on and headed outside. It was October. It was a blue-sky day, and the leaves rattled under his feet. He stopped by the tow truck and knocked the dirt off the tires and then looked at the side of the garage where the paint was peeling. He kicked at the tires again. On Saturday he'd brought Tracy, their youngest, with him, and she'd stood by the door when he locked up. She was in her jeans and had a pink sweater on that was Gabby's last year, or maybe Georgia's. Or maybe it was hers to start with and she'd already worn it thin at the elbows.

"Are the clouds making snow? Are they snow clouds yet?" she asked, and Gabe said no. Then he'd ducked her up onto his shoulders, closer to the sky, and watched her peel off a curl of paint from the side wall, and he was worried about that now—that the building really needed paint and it was too late in the year even if he had the time for scraping and painting or the money to hire somebody, which he didn't.

That was the thing, actually. Before his dad's bypass surgery, Gabe had been the help and his dad had made the decisions and paid the bills, but now it was just him by himself, just Gabe and the garage, right down to the mortgage. Lissy said he liked being the boss, and maybe he did, though it didn't mean he liked having his dad sick or liked being the one whose phone rang seven nights a week or being the person to let the girl from the high school go when she got the invoices wrong.

Since the truck had to stay, he was driving Tim's car home, and Gabe bent his head down and squeezed himself inside. The car was an ancient, sun-bleached VW that just fit if you liked your head nudged against the roof and the dashboard scrunching your knees. He moved his shoulders against the seat. He tried to get comfortable, and then he pulled out of the alley and headed off toward the bridge. It felt strange driving home this way. He was used to the big push of the truck going downhill, to the steering wheel like a rein that ran the horsepower under the hood right to him. But driving a car wasn't really like driving at all, especially a car this small that had a rattle in the back end that stood for a motor and that felt, if you thought about it, like a lid, like some kind of shell on your back.

Gabe toyed with the vent window, trying to get it tight so the air didn't whistle in. He was three stoplights from home, which was a mile and a half and all the stoplights in town, and he was thinking it would be fine if he and Lissy weren't taking this trip, if it was just him going home for lunch like he always did, home to Lissy's violin song, that song to fiddle to, and then back to work. But she was counting on this trip. She had her Avon money saved and she'd said all along it was her treat, though he'd told her he was buying the dinner. There was no way he was having her pay for a dinner in front of a whole restaurant.

They'd had it nice, actually, with all three girls in school this year. He'd drive the truck home and Lissy had lunch ready at 12:15. She could count on him coming home unless he got swamped, and he could count on things being ready when he got there. They had a regular life that way, and even before he'd get to the house he'd think he could hear it, the violin song that was Lissy's favorite rising above the great throaty vibration of the truck. Impatiently, eagerly, he'd push on the accelerator and rumble the truck on into the driveway, honking the horn once, thinking all the time of Lissy as she climbed the stairs ahead of him to the bedroom after they ate. "I suppose you want that Verdi playing again," he'd say, teasing her. "You and Giuseppe."

The first stoplight was red, but the second was yellow and Gabe went on through. He was thinking about just how close he was to the pavement. It was a little like driving under the traffic, driving a VW, but it was fun how it cornered. By the time he'd pulled into his own driveway, he was done feeling Tim needed a raise for payments on a new car. This car was all right. It was fine, in fact, and he tapped on the horn once and went around back to the porch, the way he always went. He felt good walking into the kitchen.

Lissy was standing next to the table and he smelled the soup cooking. "I tried getting you at work," she said. "Oh, Gabe."

"What?" he said, stopping. The girls flash-froze in his mind, the way they were leaving for school in the morning, and he logged it in, too, that Lissy was still in her jeans and didn't have her makeup on, that she wasn't ready to leave.

"It's your dad. He got worse, Gabe. He's real bad. No, it's more than that. Gabe, he's dead. I heard the ambulance go by and I didn't even know it, but I felt funny. Ramona called. Gabe, I'm sorry. I'm just real real sorry."

Gabe was sorting. There was Lissy's face, all tight, and the tears in her eyes. And there was her voice, which he thought was still talking to him, though her lips had trembled closed. *Gabe, he's dead. He's dead.* That's what he was hearing.

When he was supposed to be in his coat and tie holding the chair for Lissy to sit down for dinner with a river view—the stiff linen of a tablecloth brushing her knees—Gabe was on his back porch steps with the paper. He had the sports section open, and he'd read the same line over four times and he still didn't know what it said. Lissy was in the kitchen frying chicken. They'd been to the hospital and the funeral home, and when they got back, Lissy had rounded the girls up from the neighbors so they wouldn't hear about it from somebody else. Tracy had tagged in last, carrying her lunchbox and overnight case, and moping because she couldn't stay at the Jessups'. It was Lissy who told them. Gabe had wondered if he should, but Lissy was the one who'd done it once already—telling him—and he couldn't think how to say it, especially to Tracy. Besides being the littlest, she was the tomboy, the one his dad had taken out in his boat in the summer and showed where to slit the fish open and lift out the bones.

All three girls were in the kitchen with Lissy now, Georgia scraping carrots, and Gabriella and Tracy setting the table. Gabe heard scraps of their conversation, but he couldn't concentrate on that either. He was seeing his mother standing at the hospital entrance when he brought the car around. She was dazed but not crying like Ramona was—Ramona who was his half sister from his dad's first marriage to the prom queen who'd died when Tony was born—Ramona who was one big flood. It was like his mother had slipped into her widowhood already, unfurling it the moment his father's heart stopped and sealing shut a whole part of herself at 12:01.

Gabe took the paper and walked around to the front of the house. He went inside and sat down in his chair in the living room and listened and didn't listen to the kitchen chatter. He was thinking about Lissy in her nightgown that looked part sky and part jungle, about her eyes when they turned blue-green in the afternoon with the window shade down and her violin song playing on ithe tape recorder. "You'd miss it, Gabe Jones," she'd whisper, "if the women in your life weren't music lovers." Gabe didn't disagree, but he was easier with what his mother said, that tone deaf was what she got marrying a football player, that she'd had a baby with big lungs and big hands and she'd named him after a horn player, and his dad had still won him with his trucks and his boats.

Gabe pushed his hands hard against his forehead. When he thought that his dad wouldn't be in the boat in the dawn anymore, when he thought about the lantern beam shining on their fishing lures while they talked about trucks and snowmobiles, about everything they liked that made noise . . .

Gabe cleared his throat a couple of times and reached down to loosen his shirt collar. He folded the paper over and took a big breath. He felt like crying. He felt like yelling out loud that music was the wrong kind of noise, that there was a wall up, a big lit-up sign flashing "get lost" if there was music and your name was Gabe Jones. The fact was it scared him and, at twenty-nine years old and six feet four and two hundred and forty pounds, there wasn't a whole lot else that did.

Except for Lissy. He'd thought he would hurt her. He was three times her size. She was so little that from a distance she looked about twelve, though now, even if she didn't look old, up close you could see she wasn't any kid.

But it had been all right. It had always been all right—Lissy with her fingers tracing his skin and her legs curling up around him, the afternoon light from beneath the window shade falling on her face. It was even fine when she told him Tracy was his boy, that he could settle for Tracy baiting her fishing line the way his dad had taught her to, and Gabe said they'd keep her a girl, let her off the hook and try again, try for an actual boy, and Lissy said no, that he'd like the girls better anyway, he was a pushover for his girls.

The cat landed on the newspaper, and Gabe pushed it off, Lissy's nightgown drifting at the corner of his mind with an image—sudden as the cat—of Lissy bursting into study hall a minute before eight, loaded with books and dragging her clarinet case the first time he'd ever talked to her.

"You play in the band?" he'd asked, and Lissy nodded, easing the books onto her desk and sliding the clarinet case under the seat. The bell rang and she leaned over a little and whispered to him—serious, a little shy, explaining.

"I'd rather it was a violin. A clarinet's what my aunt had. She gave it to me."

And he had tried then to understand. For two years, his senior year and Lissy's, which was the first year he worked full-time for his dad who couldn't be dead—no way he was dead, Gabe couldn't stand it he was dead—for two years he'd run the tow truck out to the freeway and rebuilt car engines on weekends and gone to every concert she played in. Sometimes he'd listened hard and other times not so hard, and in the end he'd decided that her kind of music, with everybody quiet and trying not to cough, was the kind that made you either bored or uncomfortable.

"You can learn," Lissy told him. "Oh, Gabe, it's being somewhere else. Somewhere special," she said, and so he took her to a real concert, a real orchestra on their wedding trip ("You marrying that little girl with the straight-up walk?" Ramona asked), and he'd tried once more to listen hard, to tune out the engine he heard ticking out of time when the kettle drum bonged. Then he shrugged.

"What do I know, Lissy?" he said. "You just go ahead."

It was what she did, but he'd always felt that she'd wanted more. Sometimes he almost set her straight, said she shouldn't want him to understand the thing that made her what she was. As if it could be separated out somehow. As if she'd be Lissy without the music when it was all wrapped up in how he felt about her, when it was a part of her like the smell of her hair and skin, when her violin song was the "go" light like the jungle, like the sky.

Gabe closed his eyes. He felt the ache in his chest swell up, the hollowed-out track that inched up to his throat and was about his dad and was mixed up some way he didn't understand with Lissy's trip and her violin song. He couldn't see his dad's face. He could see his dad's hair, which had stayed thick and mostly brown, and he could see the way his shirt pulled at the button across his waist. But he couldn't find his face. It stayed in some colorless twilight or in an overcast dawn when the fish were biting and his dad, casting his line, was a silhouette of rasping, living breath.

The paper twitched. Gabe felt a pressure on his chest and then his eyelashes and eyelid being raised.

"You awake, Daddy?" Tracy was peering intently into his opened eye, the band of freckles wrinkled across her nose. He opened his other eye and she let his eyelashes go. "Supper's ready if you are," she said.

People were coming from all over for the funeral, and Gabe thought it was a nightmare. His parents' house was already full, and at home he and Lissy were moving into Georgia's room so his aunt and uncle could use their room when they arrived from Chicago.

"How come they can't sleep in Georgia's room?" Gabe asked when they were driving home from his mother's, and Lissy gave him a look and said something about the mattress and the space. She was tired, frazzled looking. Maybe she looked like he did. For two days they'd been calling people or had the phone ringing, and they'd been with his mother and then at Ramona's and the funeral parlor and back again with his mother. The whole time there were people coming in and out, and the dining room table at his mother's stacked up with cakes and pies and so many casseroles that might spoil that Ramona had already half-filled the freezer in the basement. On every trip back upstairs, she said how good it was it was October before deer season so the freezer wasn't full, and then she was crying again, saying she was an orphan, that two pounds of venison burger and a package of steaks were all that was left of her father's last deer. Gabe got mad finally and said what about Sonia Jones who raised her and was still plenty alive, and Lissy said there was no need fighting. That it was a strain on his mother just as it was.

When they got in the house, Gabe paid the babysitter, and Lissy went upstairs to check on the girls. He heard her in the room overhead, moving things around, and he opened a beer and stood at the back door looking out the window at the moonlight. She called him and he finished his beer, and then he climbed the stairs and went down the dark hallway past the girls' school pictures and his and Lissy's graduation photos and the rest of the family pictures. Without looking, he could see the one of his dad and Tracy holding a northern.

Gabe stuck his head in the room the girls were in. Gabby was in her own bed and Georgia was in Tracy's, and Tracy was on the floor in her sleeping bag. Lissy was talking to her, saying she was the lucky one, camping out in October, and if she'd peek out the window, she'd have the moon for a nightlight.

Which was true. The moonlight was up here, too.

"They want their kiss goodnight." Lissy got up off the floor, dusting her knees, which was just a reflex, Gabe thought, since she'd been cleaning every spare minute she'd had at home since they heard. She went past him through the door and Gabe sat down on Gabriella's bed.

"Who needs kissing?" Gabe asked and he smoothed Gabriella's soft hair against the pillow—Gabriella who was the prettiest. She looked the most like Gabe's grandmother, and Lissy always said she had perfect pitch and Gabe said whatever, she was so good looking it would have made sense anyway they'd named her after him, though of course it could have been after Lissy. It was just the dark hair he meant. Lissy didn't need to give him that look. He was kidding, all right?

She was nose down in the pillow. "Night, Gabby Face," Gabe said, pushing her hair back to kiss her cheek, and she reached up, warm and sleepy, and put her arms around his neck.

Gabe switched beds. Georgia, who'd gotten religious since the start of the school year, had her hands folded under her chin, saying her prayers. Gabe waited, half listening. Her birthday was a week from his—Lissy said she'd been his birthday present—and he always felt that for the last week in March the two of them were a whole year closer in age, nineteen years apart instead of twenty. This year she'd be ten before he turned thirty. *Thirty.*

She was the one like Lissy. She was tiny and curly-headed and the moonlight seemed to fall in arcs in her hair. She started another prayer.

"I'm not in heaven. What are you talking about?" Gabe teased, and Georgia said the Lord's Prayer was about God not fathers, but was

Grandpa in heaven and Gabe nodded yes, and pulled the quilt up over her hands.

He could hear Tracy wrestling with the sleeping bag. "How come you're not asleep?" He got down on the floor beside her.

"Have they got fish there? I don't know if he'll like it if he can't fish."

"They've got fish. They've got big ones and little ones both. They've got some with white on them you can see right through."

"Through to where?"

"You're waking me up," Gabby said from her pillow, and Gabe rolled Tracy over and patted the small rise of her bottom where it pushed the sleeping bag up.

"The next part that's white," he said. "They've got layers of white. Go to sleep now. All three of you go to sleep."

He went back down the hall. Lissy was making the bed in their room with the good sheets, and Gabe closed the door.

"We'd be back home by now anyway," she said without looking at him.

"How come you're doing that? He said midnight. It's still three hours. Two and a half." Gabe took the sheet out of her hand.

"Maybe they left early. Maybe he got off work early. I just want it done, Gabe." Lissy reached for the sheet.

Gabe stopped her hand. "What's all the hurry?" He put his arm around her. He pushed her hair back and kissed her neck. He eased his fingers up through her curls, and then reached over for the button on the tape recorder on the table by the bedside.

"What?" Lissy said. She stepped back, and then she'd moved around him and clicked the violin song off at the first note. She turned around, and there was something besides all the tiredness in her face, some edge.

"Gabe Jones. Gabe, I was hoping it would make a difference. I really was. If we got away someplace. Just someplace that was different. Special. Not this same old everyday. But we'd be home by now.

Like I said. And maybe we wouldn't have liked it." Lissy started to cry and then she choked her tears back.

"Oh, Gabe, we got these people coming I don't even know. The girls aren't asleep yet and your father's just dead and *this*. Is *this* is all you can think about ever? Honestly, Gabe Jones."

She looked over her shoulder, listening, and Gabe heard the knock at the door and the knob turning.

"You're back up?" Lissy said.

Tracy pushed the door open. "I can see through the moonlight. It's all white. Maybe it's a fish. Maybe it's a shark."

"You head right back to bed, young lady." Lissy took Tracy's hand and started out the door. "It isn't any fish," she said, but what Gabe heard was, *See Gabe? Didn't I tell you?* and he watched her walking down the hall, the straight-up line of her back, and what he'd wanted to say and hadn't was how else did she figure he could *stop* thinking? For all Ramona's carrying on, it was his dad that was gone, too. Gabe was getting these flashes in his head and right now they were all bad. Like his dad looking at him, too angry to talk when Gabe did a ring job that blew an engine. Or his dad's eyes after a game when Gabe tackled a jersey instead of a player. And the twisted look on his dad's face at the hospital—like he'd screamed himself dead.

Lissy was all business coming back into the room. She shook the sheet way up in the air so it flew near the ceiling before it landed on the bed. Gabe was mad. What was all this talk about something different? He'd said he'd go with her. He'd done all the arrangements just like she wanted. Was it supposed to be his fault that his dad died?

He moved the other sheet to the chair arm and sat down, watching her smooth out the wrinkles. For all he knew, it was a whim, Lissy getting her trip idea back in the summer when his dad had his operation and they were waiting to hear the results in the hospital lounge. She'd said they should do this for fun sometime, and Gabe thought she'd gotten a whiff of something, but she said she meant they should take a day off in the middle of the week when everybody else was working. They could get away like this to someplace different, though of course it was bad waiting to see how his dad would be. She didn't mean she liked this, though she wouldn't have missed being here with his mother and with Ramona and with Tony and Judy down from the Cities and, if the twins weren't here, that was the good news right there, that it wasn't a thing where the army would fly them in because of the seriousness. Lissy could talk a lot when she was nervous and Gabe got quiet, and that's what that had been about. But if this whole trip was just an impulse from the start, Gabe didn't know what the big deal was.

He waited a minute. "I was thinking before all this happened," he started. He stretched his legs out on the rug. "With Gabby's birthday coming up, maybe we should get her a violin. It's what you wanted. You said she's got the ear."

"Oh, right, Gabe. A violin." Lissy was tucking the corners of the sheet in, and then she was listening again. She went to the window and looked out at the driveway. "No, I know they're not here," she said, turning back, shaking him off before he could say anything. "Look, I'm sorry if I was mean. With your dad and all. I'm real tired. Listen though, Gabe. Maybe a violin's what I wanted once more than anything. But face it. That's some other people, Gabe. Somebody special. Somebody that actually deserves it that's got more imagination than you and me."

"Oh, you think so," Gabe said. He stood up. She was so small, so almost fragile, and he felt suddenly so very deep in a well of loss he couldn't find the top of.

In the morning the whole family was at Gabe's mother's before they left for the funeral home. The twins were in their uniforms, and both of them looked very fit—no triple bypasses planned on there. The two of them pummeled each other's stomachs and Andy said Luke was fat, and Luke said Andy was, but Gabe could tell firm when he saw it. Everybody looked good. His girls were getting compliments on their dresses Lissy had made in the spring in the different colors they picked. Gabe didn't remember what Georgia and Gabby said their shades were, but he knew Tracy wanted black and that's why Lissy had made hers in navy blue. They were the last ones to arrive. He'd been out to the freeway to tow a car the ambulance crew had pried two kids out of. He couldn't even talk about it when he got home. He just hurried up and got dressed.

Now he was on the couch next to Tony, his oldest brother, listening to him chew on Pepto-Bismol tablets. Tony was shaky, hung-over, and Gabe figured he'd stayed up playing cards and talking with Luke and Andy, and that he was the one who drank the beer and they were the ones that got the money.

Gabe looked at his mother. He saw her straighten her dress and do a head count and come up one short and then look puzzled before she realized who she was missing. She was doing OK. She cried some, especially when her friends came, but when she got busy, like last night when she dished out the casseroles and dessert to the kids, she seemed pretty good. She'd been worried at first there'd be a wedding at the church since they needed it for Saturday, and everybody said how good it was there wasn't. And she'd been nervous, too, about his grandmother. There was the old fight between them that came out on church occasions like this—Francesca the Catholic, who'd raised her daughter on Gregorian chants, and Sonia the Lutheran, who'd done the practical thing. Gabe knew the story. They all knew the story. At twenty-five, Sonia had gone to her mother and told her straight out she was a married woman with five children to raise, three of her own and two of George's, and the Catholics, the whole church could keep its multiplication tables to itself. After that, Francesca sang the Hallelujah Chorus at the Catholic church, and Sonia sang hers with the Lutherans, but as far as Gabe knew, his grandmother was still coming to the funeral.

"What time is it, Gabe? If we're the main show and we're paying for the limos, we better get started." Tony blew his nose and stood up from the couch. Gabe had it figured out who people were riding with so they didn't need all the cars, but Andy started directing traffic, and

Gabe just let him. They were all feeling it, all four boys, he thought—a need to step into their father's shoes, though maybe he felt it the least since he was already the one driving the truck.

At the church, Gabe helped maneuver the casket up the steps, and he didn't really think so much how the weight inside was the weight of his father next to him one last time. He was the anchorman here, the last man between the casket and the street, and he was a workingman with a job to do until they had the casket secured, until it rolled onto the floor of the vestibule.

The organ was playing. It had the whole church full of sound, and Gabe felt the sweat under his collar. He'd done this before, rolled a casket up the aisle when his grandfather died. Ten years ago. Just ten.

He followed his brothers back to the pews. Tracy was leaning out into the aisle, hanging on to the curve of the wood, waiting for him. He touched her arm, and she moved over next to Lissy, and Lissy made her stand still and not peek around at Gabby. Gabe thought he wanted Georgia next to him since she didn't squirm.

Well what he really wanted was Lissy next to him. What he wanted was to have this over before his collar choked him, but there was still the whole service to get through. He opened his program and read his father's name. *George Anderson Jones.* It was a big name, Gabe thought, a name with weight to it and nothing to mess with, which was like his dad.

"Sit by your sisters," Gabe said to Tracy, and Lissy looked up at him, surprised, but let Tracy climb on over her. The minister was in Ephesians somewhere. People were hiccoughing and blowing their noses. Gabe tried not to watch his mother's back shake. Whenever she cried, it was like she was idling fast, and Gabe always thought there was something to fix.

Tony had started clearing his throat, getting ready to make the eulogy. He'd had Gabe look through it, and Gabe wished he'd leave out the part Judy had found on a plaque in the Hallmark store, but that was the part Tony liked best. Tracy might like it, too, Gabe thought—all that business of soaring with the wild birds—but it didn't sound like his dad. His dad and birds got together with a shotgun, and that was it.

Gabe looked at Lissy out of the corner of his eye and heard Tony's birds choke in his mouth. Lissy had her new dress on—the one she'd made for the trip—and, realizing it, Gabe felt another darkness in him, crowding the black hole his dad had left.

In the night, they'd just lain there. With Georgia's mattress, Lissy was up in the air on her side of the bed, and Gabe was on a slope toward the floor. He thought she'd had her muscles tight to keep from rolling downhill—a whole night of tightened muscles keeping herself away from him.

"Gabe, wait," she'd said in the morning when he started out to the truck to go to the freeway, but when he turned around she looked at him and said, "Oh, nothing," and went back into the dining room to finish breakfast with his aunt and uncle. She'd been real nice to them. His uncle kept calling Gabe a lucky devil, and his aunt wanted to know how Lissy stayed so tiny, cooking like she did.

Gabe had an answer ready. *There's nothing special about it. She just cooks more than she eats. You don't need any imagination to figure that out.*

And he might have said it, too, said it just to watch Lissy's back go straight, but it was when the phone rang for the wrecker. And then those kids on the freeway . . . Gabe thought maybe he was losing his mind.

He reached in his pocket for his handkerchief and wiped his forehead. There wasn't a church made cool enough for a big man. They were built nearly to suffocate a person, and Gabe was wondering if he was going out right here, if his heart was kicking in and kicking him out like his father's did him. Tony came back to his pew and his shirt was half black spots. Moving spots. Gabe checked the side door, the nearest way to leave, but his breathing was getting slower. It had evened out some. He guessed he was all right. Just tired. Just really worn out.

And they were making progress. The pastor had had his say about George Jones, *a man anybody could count on*, and everybody prayed and everybody was led beside the still waters, and then Gabe saw his grandmother. She was on the other side of the aisle, off to the side, and she had a scarf on the way she always did for church. She was fidgeting around, looking behind her in the pew and getting organized the way she did when she rode in his pickup and was making sure she didn't forget something on the seat. So she was leaving early? Gabe watched her, and then looked in the program and her name was there—*Francesca Caratini Lindholm*. She was down to sing special music and Gabe wondered when his mother had asked her.

His grandmother was standing up in the pew, making her way out, her purse bumping against the end. She started down the aisle toward the back, gawking up at the balcony like the stranger she was here. An old woman. Gabe heard her footsteps in the aisle, heard them finally thumping up to the choir loft.

He listened. The organ started. It played for a moment and then the voice began, low, uncertain at first, lodged on one note. Then, all at once it swept higher, not a quaver, but the full assurance of sound carrying from the past, his infancy when his lullabies had been full of softness, of rolling "r's" —the pure voice left in an old body as good bones last in a woman's face. Gabe looked across at his grandmother's empty seat.

But Lissy had stiffened beside him. Her fingers were white, holding on to the pew back, and Gabe realized suddenly—astonished—that his grandmother's song was Lissy's song, the violin song except with words to it, Italian words, though the only ones he recognized were *Ave Maria* and *prega*.

He hadn't known they could sing the *Ave Maria* to this tune. He hadn't known it was sad this way. And not sad. And he hadn't known an *Ave Maria* was a song you could make love to, or have sung at your funeral. It was all there, every note tracing the expressions on Lissy's face when he touched her in the afternoon, when she touched him. Even the surge, the sudden shift of moods was there, and the tremor across her eyes. Gabe stared into his program, stared at the verses written in Italian and English below his grandmother's name. And below Verdi's name. *Giuseppe* Verdi. Gabe's eyes ricocheted and then blurred into focus: *Pray for us now, and in the hour of dying. Pray thou for her who is sadly sighing, as all the early hopes of bliss betray her* . . .

Gabe flinched. He was missing something, though he was feeling a glimmer. There was something about this and maybe about Lissy's trip, and he wondered all at once if Lissy had seen the words, if maybe she'd known them all along, if the thing that was special about this music wasn't that his grandmother was singing it or that it was Lissy's song right down to her skin, but something else deeper that meant she wasn't really happy when he'd thought that she was.

His mother had stopped crying to listen. Gabriella was gaping, turned around in the pew. There was a pause in his grandmother's voice while the organ held a note, and Gabe knew that part, too. But it was the next line, the sweet spot stroked again and again that he was listening for. And then, after it, the strange notes that were like a disturbance that eased into a frown and smoothed away. Gabe was hearing it all, and hearing his grandmother, in her old body, climbing to the sky with a high note and then settling back again to earth: *Amen.*

He closed his program. He was looking at his hands. They were so rough with the line of grease that would never quite scrub away around his fingernails, his middle fingers hairy below the knuckles. His dad's hands. Blunt hands to live with for every day of his life.

Lissy shifted next to him, a light motion and scent of perfume. "Gabe," she whispered. "Gabe, are you OK?"

Gabe felt her hand close tight on the clench of his fist, but he couldn't look at her. The song had stayed with him. It was beautiful. He thought he knew that. It was beautiful but it had scared him. He thought it meant something had changed. Something that wouldn't change back. Something he didn't understand that meant he'd gotten *this* close. That he'd actually touched the very hour of dying.

A Marriage in the Life of Faith Davenport

She was coming up the hill from her uncle's place, the smell of his shop still with her, that odor she'd always loved of black things—of machine oil and rubber, though she was a girl, too, who liked a scent of peach in her hair.

"Hello there, Faith. Evening."

"Evening." Through the mist of their sprinkler, she saw the neighbors in their lawn chairs and she waved, going up the sidewalk.

They *would* call her Faith. The day she died or they did, Glenn and Hazel Pritchard would, but didn't she have her friends and even her father used to Faye by now? And the Davenport was going, too. As soon as she married J. B. Truman, no more Faith Davenport. No more, "Let's have Faith on the davenport," or the rest of it that went with a name like hers.

It came to her then that she'd made up her mind. She went in the front door and sat down in the living room, which was half-dark with the shades still drawn against the heat. A cricket chirped in the corner and Faye saw it leap through the air and scuttle away behind the curtains.

"Mrs. J. B. Truman," she said out loud. "Faye Truman."

It had a flat sound, she thought. Listening to it, it was a name that disappeared in the air. It had no heat. It had no shape or noise.

Faye picked up a pillow off the couch and hugged it into her chest. All day long she'd been more than worried, knowing it was time she decided. In the kitchen baking for her aunt's church bazaar and later sweeping up in her uncle's shop while the robin with the nest over the window kept flying by the open door to squawk at her, she'd been trying to think what to do. Now it was settled. The weight of it, the decision, was lodged right in her chest behind the pillow, while the cause of it—she sighed—was threatening to show farther down.

Faye tossed the pillow away and gathered her knees up to her chest. She'd worn a rut in her mind going over the same questions again and again. All day. All week. Every hour of the four weeks since she'd known for sure, she'd hardly thought of a thing else.

She'd counted up five choices at the most. She could keep it. She could give it away. She could do something about it. Or the last two—she could tell Jamie and hope he'd do the right thing by her, or she could marry J. B. Truman.

When you thought about it hard, though, there weren't really even five.

Faye got up and opened the window shades. A moth was flitting against the glass and she swiped at it and then leaned her forehead against the pane. Any minute now her father would be back, rolling in tired from the road, the heat coming off him the way it did from his rig. There he'd be still choking from two weeks of road dust.

And she was supposed to try it on him to keep a baby here? Fat chance she could hand him his beer and say, "Well Daddy, next year there'll be two of us, one bawling, to welcome you home."

No way. Not a prospect in the world she'd do that, and so there it was. Raising a baby in this house wasn't any choice. And neither was giving it away. She couldn't see herself doing that at all, once it was a fact, a baby right there. And as far as getting rid of it went, all she could see in her mind was her mother somewhere in the clouds in eternity, still stuck in bed as if she'd never died her way out of it, and saying, "Now Faith honey, where *is* this grandchild they told me about?"

No, what those three were, were impossibilities, not choices, and what it left her with was Jamie and J. B.

That was what she'd done her wrangling over. She'd gone round and round about it, talking to herself all day. It was like tossing and turning without the bed. She'd think of Jamie, and the sense of love that swept over her was so excruciating she had to hold her breath to keep from shaking. How could he even exist the way he was, as perfect as he was? And if she'd studied his face a thousand times, didn't it surprise her still to discover herself there, reflected in his eyes, the pale, sharp blue of his irises surrounding her—lovestruck, lovesick. Oh, Jamie. In her mind, she wound her fingers in his curls again and matched her walk to his, Jamie with the stretchy body browned all over to the white mark of his swim trunks, stuck on him like a paper cutout.

Faye crossed her arms and pinched her shoulders until they hurt. And then there was J. B., of course, J. B., who couldn't stop staring at her so it showed he loved her like it was written on him. J. B. Truman would marry her in a minute, regardless, and he'd have what he wanted.

The moth came back, diving into the window, and Faye saw it flutter, a little blur of movement that was like the bigger blur in her mind of Jamie and J. B., fused together somehow like a photograph that was double exposed.

But what harm was it she'd do J. B. Truman? Wasn't he old enough to know his own mind? Two tours of duty at least he'd done in Vietnam with the medics and now he'd worked on the ambulance crew at home twelve years, and what harm could he do to her, a man as soft and steady and good as he was? He was like a big St. Bernard, J. B. was, that just went around saving people.

Faye put her hand over the moth and felt it beating against her palm and the windowpane. She was saving somebody, too. She knew she was. Wasn't that the point of the whole thing and what she'd convinced herself about finally? She was saving Jamie for school and for whatever he wanted to do for the whole rest of his life, and she was saving herself from waking up someday to find out he hated her.

Faye stared down at her hand and then slowly spread her fingers apart and watched the moth spurt out and flutter away. She could hear a rumble now and, looking up, she spotted her father's truck cab down at the corner, nosing up to the stop sign.

Well there he was and here she was. She had maybe one minute to get out a beer and set the table and see if the sausage was still good and if she had enough ice cream in the carton, and maybe she had thirty seconds more to figure out just how she'd tell him she was marrying J. B. Truman anytime now and still going for a walk with Jamie when he got off work tonight at ten.

In the kitchen, hurrying, she knocked the saltshaker off the counter and the plug came out so the salt spilled all over the floor in front of the stove. She was still sweeping up when her father came in from the back porch.

"Something burning?" he said.

Faye looked at the stove and then at him, at his red nose and his squinty, tired eyes. She shook her head.

"So where's my beer?" Her father sat down heavily at the table, his stomach settling in stages after him, and Faye got a beer from the fridge and popped the top, and watched him drink it down.

"Your trip good?" she said.

Her father leaned on his beer can. "Came back half empty," he said. "If you call that good."

"It's been real hot here." Faye was spooning sauerkraut onto the sausage and she nudged the stringy part back up under the bread, waiting until she knew there wasn't any more answer coming. Sometimes she could do what her mother had—tiptoe around his tiredness and crankiness until the beer smoothed things out. But all she could think about right now was that it *was* hot and she hadn't even opened the windows upstairs to get the air moving in the bedrooms.

"Be back in a minute. Here." She put the plate with the food on it down on the table and set out another beer, and then she went out quickly and headed for the stairs.

It was musty going up. It was stuffy and it got hotter and hotter. Faye trailed her hand along the wallpaper and rounded the corner into the upstairs hall. It was hot enough, she guessed, for a person to suffocate and the air was stale besides. She pushed up the window at the end of the hall and then opened all the windows, banging through the bedrooms.

For a moment she sat on the sill in her own room. It was her Aunt Lily's doing that she slept down the road with them and had her meals there when her father was gone. It was her aunt's idea, too, for Jamie to pick her up there and her idea, if Hazel Pritchard needed any encouragement, to keep Glenn and Hazel spying to see if she and Jamie came back here.

They could save their time. Faye got up and went back out in the hall, sniffing past her parents' room. How could anyone that knew her think she'd bring Jamie here? What would she do?—come pulling him by the hand up the stairs to this mustiness and the smell of holy water going sour in the dish by her parents' room where her mother had died? It was an idea that rotted away, just thinking of it, like some maggoty fruit that fell apart when you touched it. Thanks, but no thanks. She'd stick to her chances on the back roads and in the back seats of cars. She *had* stuck.

Faye pushed the curtains back from the hall window and then went downstairs. Her father had the ballgame on and he was eating ice cream and his cigarette was burning on the edge of his plate.

"That rookie—the hot one—what's his name. He just hit a home run. You got more ice cream?"

"I can get some."

"I guess I had enough." Her father leaned back, his hands behind his head, and he'd revived some, she could tell. "So what you been up to, honey?"

"Not a whole lot." Faye got down on her knees hunting in the cabinet under the sink for the cleanser and, with the water going, she started scrubbing on the skillet. "We got the baking done for Aunt Lily's bazaar."

She sounded funny. She thought she did, and she kept scrubbing harder and harder and her hair fell down across her face. She brushed it back with her hand.

"So when's this bazaar?"

"Friday."

"You getting in thick with the Lutherans?"

"Well Aunt Lily . . ." Faye stopped. Her hands were shaking in the skillet. They were shaking so hard that the water in the skillet was spattering into the sink. "Daddy, I'm marrying J. B. Truman," she said, and she stared straight ahead at the wallpaper over the sink and listened for him to answer something, anything, but all she could hear was the announcer on the radio saying the balls and strikes.

"Me and J. B.," she stared again.

"I heard you."

Faye rinsed the skillet off and dried it and turned around. "I was thinking we'd do it in August."

"This one coming in three weeks? August?"

"Yes."

Her father pushed his cigarette out on the plate, and then he lit another one. He was coughing. "And it's J. B.," he said.

"You like J. B. It won't cost much. Just for the buns and cake. I got Grandma's dress."

"You're marrying J. B. Truman."

"I *am* old enough. I'm almost eighteen and you know how good J. B. is and he's got his own place."

"What about Jamie Squires? Jamie been stepping out on you?"

"No." Faye pulled a chair out from the table and sat down. Her father was looking right at her, a dark stare through the smoke of his cigarette, and he didn't look squinty-eyed or tired anymore.

"Faye, you got something to tell me?"

"I did tell you." She rolled the edge of the oilcloth up in her fingers. "I want it the first week in August if we can get the church."

"You know what I mean." He was looking at her hard, as hard as he ever had, but there was still, too, an expression in his eyes of that sadness and perplexity that had never really left him since her mother's death and Faye seeing it, feeling it, had a sudden intense hope, a desire to go ahead and tell him everything.

She sat still, her knees locked hard against the chair, and in waves that came over her like heat, she thought of Jamie. She was almost ready to say something.

"All right." Her father stood up from his chair and moved over to the sink. "He's a good man, J. B. I can give you a car. You'll need a car."

Faye stared up at him, at the sweat staining his shirt between his shoulder blades and at the bald spot on his head. "Jamie's coming. I didn't tell him yet," she said. She looked down at the tablecloth. She heard her father behind her, filling a glass of water at the sink and drinking it. "A car would be good."

"Maybe Jeff'll know one. He and Lily going up to the lake again?"

"Not this week." Faye put her hands on the table and stood up. "I'm getting ready," she said. "You need anything else?"

Her father shook his head. He was still standing with his back to her at the sink, his glass in his hand, and Faye kissed him quickly on the shoulder seam of his shirt and slipped out and upstairs and, when she came back down a half an hour later, he was asleep on the couch with the TV on and the newspaper over his chest.

She waited for Jamie on the back porch with her sandal stuck in the ivy on the railing. It was still hot and a leftover June bug buzzed her and then hit the kitchen window, going for the light.

Jamie was humming when he came up. "I got the car out front. You rather go for a ride?" he said. He leaned against the railing and then he wrapped his fingers around her ankle and lifted her foot out of the ivy. "That car'd cool you off."

"No." Faye shook her head and stood up. She was tempted all right. She knew she was. Somehow, though, breezes or no breezes, a ride didn't really seem like the proper thing anymore. "Let's just walk," she said. She stuck her hands in her pockets, and Jamie gave her a funny look, but he didn't say anything.

Out front they turned right, heading up past Pritchards' and the edge of town. It was cooler walking, Faye decided. She slipped her sandals off and hooked them over her finger. There were lightning bugs in Pritchards' yard, and Jamie caught one while she walked on the edge of the grass where it was still wet from the sprinkler. She looked in Jamie's hands at the lightning bug turning green.

"It thinks you're a jar," she said. She put her hand on his fingers.

"It's the color Ted Raffin was at Klemper's. He got real lit up."

"He would."

They were past Pritchards' now and there were more fireflies ahead of them, blinking and sailing along the road. Faye pulled her sandals back on and felt her feet squish in wet against the leather. She could hear cars in the distance, roaring around at the racetrack, and there was a din of crickets and the thick smell of dying peonies. A horse whinnied softly in a field.

"You fry a lot of hamburgers?" Faye said.

"I did." Jamie reached over and caught her hand and swung it in his. "A lot of French fries, too. We going down to the river here?"

"All right."

Faye hesitated, even though she'd answered. She wasn't sure. Not quite, though what harm was it, really, heading for the river one last time? They could curl their legs over the bank and see the moonlight shining on the water. "All right," she said again.

Jamie led the way. The river path veered off from the road through a thicket of trees that grew down the hillside, and Faye leaned into his shoulder to keep the branches from slapping her in the face. Pebbles crunched under her sandals.

"We'll go listen for an owl," Jamie said. He squeezed her hand.

"Can you feel moonlight? What is it—is it cold or warm?" Faye listened for an owl and heard the river. She heard the rush of it in the darkness.

"Maybe a dog feels it to howl. I don't know."

They were at the riverbank, the black trees hanging above them and the sky a faint purple to the north from the lights of town. Faye found a rock at her feet and tossed it into the water, exploding the moon's reflection.

She sat down. Jamie sat down and maybe they listened. Faye thought they did, but she was thinking besides. She bent the toe of her sandal back against the creek bank and, with Jamie's arm around her and his breathing following hers like an echo, she dreamed a daydream in the dark about living in sunlight and having Jamie always there. She was thinking of picnics and baseball games and Jamie cannonballing into the swimming pool from the high dive, and it smelled like hot dogs where her mind was (though maybe that came from the just perceptible scent of food Jamie had cooked at work), and it smelled like ice cream, too. There was this fat baby trying to eat an ice cream cone in a stroller while she and Jamie giggled over it.

What it was she wanted to know was how that baby looked, but with Jamie there beside her and peering into the stroller in her mind, the face just wouldn't come clear. Faye squinted her eyes shut trying to see, but all she felt was frightened. Somehow with Jamie in the picture, that baby didn't really look like anybody at all, and least of all like Jamie the way she knew it had to.

"You're real quiet."

Faye started and opened her eyes. "You hear your owl yet?"

"Jumpy, too. What owl?" Jamie's arm got tighter around her and he was kissing her neck, and Faye knew she was in the wrong place even if it felt like someplace wonderful instead. She pulled away.

"Jamie it's hot and I've got that dust in me still from sweeping up at Uncle Jeff's and I'm marrying J. B. like he wants me to and I have to go." She stood up, her whole speech rattled off in a second and a half, and when she looked down at Jamie she realized he hadn't heard a word she'd said.

"Oh, Jamie," she said, her voice just dying away on itself in her throat. She could see his eyes with the moonlight caught in them, and he was leaning back, all lazy, on his elbow.

"I'm going," she said. She started back up the path, and the tree branches scratched her in the face. She was running up the hill, tripping on the stones and weeds, and then she heard him coming, too, a thudding sound on the path behind her, a sound like an animal breaking through the underbrush. She wanted to wait. With all she was, she wanted to stop still until he caught her, but she kept on going, fleeing from him and the thought of them together, gnarled in the tree branches.

~

On her wedding day, Faye Davenport woke up with the lawn mower going in the yard and a patch of sunshine warming her foot where it stuck out of the sheet. She blinked her eyes open. It had rained in the night, rained and then blown hard and now, even with the sunlight turning her curtains golden, the room seemed cool.

Faye pulled the sheet up. Really, it was cool. It was like those mornings at the lake when the wind went through the pines and you shivered on the dock and then plunged into shock-cold water.

It was hardly, though, what she'd expected for August. Faye stretched and pushed her pillow back behind her head and stared. Her wedding gown was hanging on the closet door, its train drifting out across the rug, and the bridesmaids' dresses were behind it, ballooning out from the clothes tree in plastic bags. She closed her eyes, putting the whole thing together again, wondering if she'd gotten it right: yellow dresses with tiny sprigs of white, bouquets of yellow and white flowers and of cornflower blue.

The lawn mower got louder, going by downstairs beneath her window, and Faye got up and pulled her slippers on and went over to her dresser. She had time still. Time to *take* her time. She could back up and stand at the window and she could rub the rough organdy of her curtains against her cheek while the birds sang in the tree outside. She could rock slowly in her rocker.

Yet things had started now. Somewhere in her head a clock was ticking down, and she meant to get on with it, to cross through everything on her list until she actually was married.

She was done with her shower, and she was eating cereal at the kitchen table in her robe and the brand-new underwear from Aunt Lily's shower when her father came in from mowing the grass.

"They get enough of those?" Her father pointed to the counter, which was full clear to the end with plastic bags stuffed with buns. He splashed water on his face and drank a big glass of orange juice. "I got the back done," he said, looking out the window, and then he went outside again. Faye watched him while she washed his glass and her bowl and spoon. The birds were yammering at him and they dive-bombed him when he mowed around the rose bushes.

By nine fifteen, the kitchen was full. Hazel's daughter-in-law, Mary, was working on Faye's hair and Faye was trying to keep her head still under the curling iron while Hazel made coffee and Candy Halfacre, who was maid of honor, perched on a cleared spot on the counter and passed out the doughnuts she'd brought. Jeri and Alice, the cousins who were bridesmaids, had gotten their bouquets from the living room and were holding them for Faye's inspection, the ribbons streaming down their jeans.

Faye nodded her head. "Hold on a minute, Davy," she said to Candy's nephew. "One more curl and we'll get your flower and your ring pillow. Here comes Aunt Lily."

"You aren't dressed yet?" her aunt said, coming in the door. Her hair was lacquered immobile in a big pile of curls on top of her head, and her face grew more flushed as she maneuvered into a chair next to Faye. "I finally found the garter. You need something blue. You think I could eat one doughnut on my niece's wedding day?"

"Help yourself," Faye said. She got herself disentangled from the curling iron and took Davy's hand. In the living room, Hazel was leaning over the couch eyeing the flower box, and Faye undid the plastic wrap on a boutonniere and pinned it on Davy.

"Don't rub the petals off," Hazel said. "Where's your father, Faye? Somebody get Sid so he can take the men's flowers to the church."

"He can't. He's taking me." Faye touched her own bouquet and took out her dad's flower and then put the lid on the box while Hazel got on the phone to call Glenn.

Faye heard the back door open and close, and Cindy, the flower girl, came tiptoeing into the room after her mother. "Aren't you perfect?" Faye said, leaning over to give her a hug. She could hear the girls moving across the floor overhead, getting dressed in her room, and she felt a touch of queasiness as if she'd eaten one of the doughnuts, though she hadn't.

Her Aunt Lily had blocked out the light in the doorway. "Faye, you'll be late to your own wedding. I told your dad to take his suit down to our house to get changed."

"In a minute," Faye said. "Davy, you want to show Cindy the presents?" Faye steered both children into the dining room, to the pots and pans and the dishes with the sunflowers in the middle that Hazel wished she had for her own kitchen and to the "His" and "Hers" towels and the American eagle placemats that Faye had already promised herself she wouldn't use in a hundred years. She straightened the bow on Cindy's dress and smelled how clean she smelled. "You two just go on and look," she said.

Upstairs in her bedroom, there was a mixed odor of fingernail polish and somebody's perfume that was spilled. Candy Halfacre was putting her sandals on, and Alice was zipping up Jeri's dress.

"One more doughnut and this wouldn't fit. Hold your breath, Jeri. What if it pops while you're going up the aisle?"

"Don't say that." Faye took her robe off and lifted her dress down from the door. It was heavy in her arms, and the girls helped her with it, tipping the skirt up over her head. Faye ducked inside. She swam up into a cream-colored rattly light and then pulled her way out through the armholes and neck and straightened the folds.

"Faye Davenport, if you don't look like a dream."

"It is real pretty, isn't it?" Faye looked in the mirror while the girls did her back up. The dress was sheeny and smooth with lace curving down below her throat and angling off into the train. She didn't think that she showed. "It's *peau de soie*," she said, and she wasn't sure that she recognized herself. She looked too blue-eyed and honey-blonde, too golden from the summer and too right in this dress to be the skittery, pale girl she felt inside.

"I'm scared," she said, and the girls laughed and Candy hugged her, bending carefully around the lace.

"Don't forget the sleeves. You're lucky it's not hot." Mary Pritchard picked up the two long tubes of lace with buttons on them and pulled first one and then the other up Faye's arms and fastened them beneath the sleeve caps on the dress. She buttoned them tight along Faye's forearms. "I guess that's the prettiest wedding dress I ever saw. And I liked mine. Let me get your hair fixed again and we'll do the veil."

Faye stood with her eyes half closed, feeling the pull of the curling iron and the brush along her neck. The veil was beautiful. It was wonderful, with handmade ivory lace along the edge, but she'd worried that it went too far, that from plain decency and her memory of her mother, she should have settled for flowers in her hair.

"Careful." Candy had the veil and Mary was giving directions, a brush in her hand. "Watch out for her hair. Careful."

Faye had the whole picture in the mirror: the girls in their yellow dresses and Mary with bobby pins in her mouth and somebody who was supposed to be Faye Davenport in all this gorgeous fabric and lace and an air-filled puff of veil. She turned a little from side to side, turned around and looked over her shoulder.

"You girls ready?" Her Aunt Lily, out of breath from the stairs, was peering in the door. "I just got frosting off Davy and sewed up Cindy's skirt where she stepped on it. Faye, wouldn't your mother like to see you though. You got the necklaces?"

"I do," Faye said, but she felt a little start of surprise. "I don't think I'd forget." She lifted the veil back and went over to her dresser and opened a drawer. "We need Cindy." She stood a minute watching while the girls opened up their boxes and hooked on their lockets with the pearls on them. Then she went downstairs, her dress swishing wall to wall, and put Cindy's locket on her herself.

Her aunt had followed her down. "How long does it take your dad to shower? If you were Lutheran I'd at least know where things are at the church." Faye nodded and went into the living room to look at the flowers once more. She stared at her bouquet, at the perfect roses and the bachelor's buttons and at the fuzzy old purple velvet of the couch covers, and a part of her wanted just to push the flowers aside and lie right down and bury her face in the velvet.

They were all carrying buns and flowers when they left the house. Faye watched her father coming across the lawn in his tuxedo.

"You're real good looking," she said, and he looked at her with his face still hot while she pinned his flower on, and then he kissed her so gently on the forehead she thought she would cry.

At the church, Hazel hurried off to find Glenn while Faye's father parked the car and Candy helped Faye with her train. In the vestibule, her Aunt Lily sniffed looking in at the bride's room.

"I can see why you wanted to get dressed at home. This little matchbox. Tina Vonns married her fireman here and her dress was wrinkled."

"I smell coffee," Faye said. She was trying to keep her teeth from chattering.

"They're already cooking downstairs. Did I say we peeled four hundred potatoes? I always thought Tina married Jerry Raffin just so she could ask him when he gets home where was the fire."

The organ was playing and Faye still smelled coffee and she thought of all the church ladies downstairs with sweat in the trace of their mustaches. "Is it time to line up yet?"

"It's a minute to. Everybody got your flowers?" Her aunt was straightening sashes. "Put your veil down, Faye. Candy, help her put it down. I'm leaving."

The organ got louder with the door open all the way and Faye held her flowers tight and followed Candy out into the vestibule. A light went off in her face.

"What's that?" she said, starting and catching onto her father's arm, and then she remembered her Aunt Lily had found somebody to take pictures.

"Hold it right there." The photographer pointed his camera sideways, and Faye tried smiling and smiling until he went on in, down to the sanctuary.

"I can't feel my feet," she whispered. Her father was clearing his throat and coughing. He took his handkerchief out and wiped his forehead.

"You look real beautiful, like your mother," he said. He was staring straight ahead, and the music got louder and Jeri was already up at the front of the church and Alice was past the back pews. Faye held her breath while Candy started and then turned back, beckoning for the children to come after her. Faye felt her father's hand on hers and she took one half step feeling her way, and then another slightly surer one forward.

When it was she saw J. B. first she wasn't sure. Things were registering out of place. She saw Tina Raffin's little girl kicking her foot against the kneeler. The altar candles were lit. Faye knew they were, but she blinked when all the camera flashes went off and she was sure for a second that the candles went out. Maybe she saw J. B.

Faye counted rows. She counted steps. She could see Hazel wiping her eyes and her Aunt Lily in the next row up. She saw the groomsmen and the best man and Father Kincaid. Then, out of everything, out of all the people and the scent of flowers and the gust of air that came up the aisle and lifted her veil, she found J. B. stuck in behind the photographer and with his hair all slicked down so she hardly knew him—J. B. finally and for sure, and waiting to get married.

Faye was past the front pew and she stopped walking. What she was worried about was making the switch—her father's arm for J. B.'s. She had visions of the two of them tangled up in her train and J. B. pitching over the altar railing. Her father squeezed her hand and then he'd stepped back just fine and she was standing with J. B. and his arm was like a rock. She could smell his aftershave.

For a moment she panicked, looking up to see if his beard was gone, but it was there, as black and curly as ever and only his neck a little chafed where he'd shaved and trimmed himself neat. She was staring at his neck and he turned and she ran into his eyes, which were still like deer's eyes, as dark and soft and open as they were, and yet somehow never any surprise in a man like J. B. was, who had no false qualities.

The singer was in the middle of "O Beautiful Mother" and Faye thought the sound was floating right down from the top of the church to wrap her up. She felt sleepy, and she clamped her mouth tight so she wouldn't yawn. Then Father Kincaid was talking and J. B. had her hand and she could feel the soft curl of his hair where it grew below his knuckles. She held on tight, listening, trying to listen, and then it was her turn to talk and her voice came out wobbly and as high as Cindy's.

"I will," J. B. said, looking at her so she could feel it, and then she said she would, too, in a little squeak, and they were married, married just like that in a done thing with only the finishing, long blur of the Mass and the music still floating to surround her in the stained light of the windows.

Outside in the receiving line, J. B. kissed her and the wind blew her veil and the sunlight fell in spots on her dress. She was happy. She thought she was, shaking hands and getting hugged to death.

"What a perfect day!"

Her Uncle Jeff said it. Hazel said it while she was speaking to Glenn, and two hundred other people said it, too, after they got done ribbing J. B. and he'd laughed about almost forgetting his name when he said his vows. Every single person loved her dress.

Then there was the license to sign, and J.B., with his wallet out, thanking Father Kincaid, and pictures and more pictures. Finally they were downstairs in the basement with the women running in and out of the kitchen, and all the coffee pots with their red lights on.

"That's a mountain of potato salad," Faye said. She looked at the glass plates full of ham on buns and the dishes with the pink and green bonbons that J. B.'s landlady had made. People were sitting at the tables, talking and waiting, and she and J. B. made their way up to the head table to cut the cake.

Somebody at one of the tables said the photographer looked like he'd just gotten out of jail, and Faye could hear her Aunt Lily and Hazel arguing behind her about coffee and the church and then Hazel saying what did Lutherans know about weddings anyway, which Faye knew was good for a six months' fight at least, and then the photographer was back and the church ladies were motioning for Faye to feed J. B. the cake. Cindy had a plate of fruit salad with little marshmallows in it all over her shoes.

When they got to Klein's for the party afterward, all Faye wanted to do was sit at the bar by the pool table with her veil and her shoes off and drink a root beer.

"I don't know what I'd do if it was hot," she told Art Klein when he poured her root beer, and he said she sure had a nice day and he and his sons kept mixing drinks and opening beer cans as fast as they could.

The band started playing and somebody got J. B. to do the Russian dance with his arms crossed and his feet kicking out from under him. The music was so fast his beard was flying, and two of the ushers tried joining in and one of them fell over backward into the pool table.

Faye was laughing and she almost spilled her root beer on her dress, but she moved in time and it got on Tarr Hansen instead, who'd just sat down beside her, and he stood up in a hurry with a big wet spot on the front of his pants.

For a minute, Faye thought she'd started a riot. People were hooting and yelling at Tarr and slapping him on the back and making crude remarks she guessed they thought were fine now she was a married woman, but the band switched to "What're You Doing the Rest of My Life?" and everybody simmered down and started clapping for her to dance with J. B.

"You want to?" he said. Faye nodded and got her shoes back on and draped her train over her arm and they started out, with J. B. humming just off-key in his deepest voice that was so low she thought it went down to the last note on the piano.

"Everybody, too," he said, waving his arm in his way that was friendly and shy at the same time, and the pool table and the card tables got moved way back and, with the dance floor full, the lead guitar player went into a solo. Faye thought she'd just like to listen, but they were cutting in already, her Uncle Jeff first and then a whole line of other people and she gave up on anything but dancing.

Sometime about four o'clock she got a chance to sit down for more than thirty seconds. Art Klein was putting out bowls of popcorn on the bar and some of the tables, and he got her another root beer and a chair.

"You sharing that?" Glenn Pritchard said, coming up, and Faye nodded.

"There's another chair over there."

"I'm not sitting. I sit once and Hazel'll find me to chew me out some more." Glenn took a handful of popcorn and then another bigger one and moved past the tables toward the bar. Faye watched him go and it came to her like a sudden shot that she was J. B. Truman's wife, Faye Truman, and she felt something chilly on the back of her neck that was like the dribble from a popsicle or an ice cream cone.

Faye stuck her straw into her root beer glass. It was all right. *She* was all right. Last night at ten thirty her father had looked at her and said, "Honey, it's not too late. You can quit anytime before tomorrow," and she'd looked straight back at him without a wobble and now, right now he was there by the bar with his beer can and his face still red and he was grinning and as happy as she'd seen him since before her mother died and leaning on something you wouldn't think he could, like the smoke from Tarr Hansen's cigarette, like maybe just the afternoon, and here she was, Mrs. J. B. Truman who'd thrown her bouquet, and there was J. B., too, who'd tossed the garter, J. B. being Mr. Polite to everybody's cousins.

Faye stood up and grabbed at her train and went across the floor. "You're real good to me, J. B.," she said in a rush, and he looked at her and then he put his arm around her so they were dancing again. It was slow music and Faye stuck her face into his shoulder so she didn't have to think or see anybody.

They had the money dance then. Ted Raffin put five dollars down her back and went off in the hallway that went to the ladies' room with Candy Halfacre, and was kissing her up against the wall.

"Sing something, Jeri," people were yelling and finally Jeri did, standing in front of the band and carrying a tune like she wasn't even J. B.'s cousin. Faye danced with her father; she danced with Jay Pritchard while Mary glared at him, and then J. B. caught her eye and she managed to duck out behind the bar to the house so she could change.

When she came back from Sue Klein's bedroom, Faye could see J. B.'s truck out front with paint and streamers on it and tin cans.

"You ready?" J. B. said, looking at her in her going-away dress that was rosy pink and soft, and Faye nodded and they both ducked their heads, with the rice flying, and ran through a whole crowd of friends and relatives toward the truck, and then detoured at the last second to her new car that nobody knew about but her father and her Uncle Jeff, who said it was good and clean and ran fine, and who'd kept a secret for once in his life. J. B. backed out fast before Ted Raffin could get his spray paint, and everybody else was yelling and laughing, and somebody was setting off firecrackers.

Then it was just the two of them driving up the road, J. B. fiddling with the radio and Faye with her hands folded in her lap, wondering if she should've worn flowers on her dress.

"You hungry?" J. B. said in a while, and it occurred to Faye maybe she was too dressed up for where they were going, that maybe

J. B. meant to catch her a fish for supper since they were staying the week at his cabin on the river. But he had a suit on, didn't he?

"You ever eat lobster, Faye?" he said.

"I don't know. I don't think so," she answered, and then *she* fiddled with the radio and they went under the interstate, heading north.

Just past Teebo Lake, J. B. stopped at a restaurant Faye didn't even know was there.

"We're eating at this place?" she said. She felt a little uncertain, out of her territory, and when J. B. opened the door for her it occurred to her to tell him to bring her something, that she'd eat in the car. She got out instead. The sun was still high. It looked cool behind the trees and she could hear the sound of an outboard motor coming from the lake.

Inside the restaurant Faye waited for J. B. by the cash register while he got a table. He was talking to a waitress and Faye could see his beard moving with his mouth. He looked nice, she thought. There was something sweet and good about J. B. that showed, and he wasn't a bit fat and some people might even say he was nice looking. And besides, here when she'd thought they'd go fishing for supper or end up somewhere with a row of trucks out front and a sign in the window for homegrown beef and Wisconsin cheese, J. B. had brought her to a place that had real tablecloths and he was talking about lobsters.

What he ordered besides was champagne and Faye kept feeling for her purse with her foot, wondering if the waitress would ask for her I.D.

"Just taste it," J. B. said and, with the bubbles in the back of her nose, Faye decided *maybe* she could get used to it—to the lobster and even the champagne—but she didn't know who in the world would believe a man like J. B. Truman had such fancy ideas about getting married.

Afterward, north on the river at his cabin, he was more J. B. He put his jeans on and a plaid shirt and he found a flannel shirt for her, too, since she hadn't packed anything warm but her best sweater. He waited for her on the porch while she changed.

"It's real calm. The wind's gone," he said, and Faye wished it was eighty degrees. She felt like swimming in the river, just sliding right down into the current with her arms over her head and then kicking up again onto her back. She poked with her foot, hunting for the loose board she'd tripped on when J. B.'d brought her here before, but there was new wood. The porch was solid.

"We taking the canoe out?" she said. She looked toward the dock and she thought of J. B. in the water, his legs white from only swimming when he had to, and she wanted to lean against his back, to touch him like the best and easiest friend she'd ever had, but they were married now. It was something different, and she stood without talking while he reached out and turned up the shirt cuffs at her wrists. His fingertips were damp, his eyes on her wrists the way he loved her face.

"Sure," he said. "If you want. I got the paddles in the shed."

On the river, and then on the creek, they drifted with the current. The sky was turning rosy. "I could fall asleep," Faye said. She let her hand trail in the water and then turned it back and forth, cold in the sunlight. There were gnats flying at the water's surface and electric blue dragonflies hovering just out of reach like a squadron of tiny helicopters.

"We could've gone fishing." Faye looked over her shoulder, and J. B. nodded, holding his paddle against the stern, turning them with the creek bank. Faye stared past him at a flying bird, small with arrow-like, darty wings and a palish-yellow, rounded stomach. J. B. pointed with his paddle. An eagle was swooping at the water from the sky, and beyond it, near the shore, a brown duck flapped into the long grass. Faye watched. Beneath the sky, the water had turned red and in the shallows she could see weeds spreading below the water like blown-over, discarded Christmas trees.

"It's real peaceful. It's nice here," she said. They were floating, gliding down beneath the sandstone cliffs of the shoreline, below leaning trees and knotted vines and through shining reflections that bent in the water, the sun warm in a blaze of descent. J. B. talked fishing.

Faye asked him questions and she guessed he told her about every kind of fish he'd ever caught here. Then he was quiet.

It was dark when they pulled the canoe back up onto the land. Faye could hear the water against the dock.

"There's a light," J. B. said. He pointed toward the cabin and the dim square of yellow beyond the porch.

Faye started up the steps. "You want a fire?" She was reaching over, gathering kindling as she went, and J. B. came up behind her with the paddles under his arm.

Inside, she sat on the floor and watched him make the fire and waited for him to sit down beside her, to start off like Jamie would, leaning back first and then stretching out with his head in her lap and looking at her and running his hand down her face and neck. Faye bit her lip.

She wasn't thinking about Jamie anymore. She was done with that. She was J. B. Truman's wife, and she wasn't scared and she wasn't really shy and even if Jamie'd made everything happen so fast she could hardly even understand, this time she figured she knew what to expect.

But he was still standing there, J. B., looking at the fire, which was burning dimly orange with little flickers of light going up the chimney.

Faye cleared her throat. "You see Cindy with those marshmallows on her shoes?"

"I did. Sure." J. B. looked back at her and then he poked at the fire and he got busier doing something with the grate.

Faye uncrossed her legs and pulled at the ring on her finger and wondered if something was wrong. Even if J. B. wasn't any talker when you weren't talking fishing, he seemed quiet to her now in a way that wasn't like him. She straightened her jeans leg. Maybe he was nervous. Maybe he was worried somehow or even having second thoughts about what she'd told him three weeks ago. Faye stood up. "You all right, J. B.?" she said.

He took a minute answering and then he said, "The draft's not right. It won't catch right," and Faye figured she had her answer, though she still wasn't sure. She was tired all of a sudden, really worn out, and she felt like crying or chewing her fingernails.

"I'm getting ready for bed," she told him. Her shoes were off and she carried them into the bedroom where J. B. had left her suitcase, and when she was done in the bathroom and had on the nightgown her Aunt Lily had sewn the lace on, she got in the bed under the sheet and counted the cracks between the boards in the ceiling. She could hear J. B. out in the living room, closing up, and she thought that anytime he'd be there, his eyes shining in the dark and his beard pressing on her neck while he moaned in her ear.

He was at the door then. She was waiting and he was waiting and then he came on in and went to the bathroom, and Faye studied the furniture, the rug, the things that looked like J. B. had them from a thrift sale, though she knew they were really from his grandmother when she died, just like the cabin.

Finally he was back. He put his jeans and shirt on the chair in the corner and she thought he was getting in bed, but then he went off to the bathroom again and a story flashed through Faye's mind about a man Glenn Pritchard had heard of that shot himself from pure fright at getting married and then wound up with a coffin delivered instead of a bed. She was almost up, ready to knock on the bathroom door, but here was J. B. coming back again.

"You OK, J. B.? You feel all right?" she said. She wanted to help, to do something to make things easier than this—to bring back the good, solid J. B.—but she had no idea of what he needed. He sounded strange. His breathing was off and when she reached for his hand his skin felt clammy.

"Faye," he said. She thought her hand would break in his. "I got something to tell you," he said, and he was gray in the face and he was off again, back in the bathroom, and Faye guessed he was sick and she thought she'd burst out laughing from plain surprise, just shriek right out how there was nothing he could say to her to compare to what she'd already told him. But she stayed still.

Anyway, she had an idea now of what was happening. Faye pushed her heels down against the bed. She'd heard what men did was tell you on your wedding night about all they women they'd been with before and then make love to you while you felt wretched—like you were connected up that way to a crowd or the whole world. Maybe J. B.—maybe even J. B. Truman had a story for her like that, and it was making him sick from his nerves. Faye felt low and dismal thinking he did, but she knew well enough she hadn't any right to. Not after Jamie.

She pulled the sheet up tight under her chin and rolled her eyes around in her head the way her mother had taught her to do when they got tired. The bathroom door was open and then the light went out and J. B. was back again and this time he seemed better.

"Sorry," he said in a low voice, and Faye waited for something more, an explanation maybe like the lobster being off, but it didn't come and she realized, with the bed sinking down beside her when he got in, that she was on the wrong track looking for excuses from J. B. Truman.

"I said I got something to tell you and I do." J. B. had her hand and he pulled it over and held it on his chest like it was a decoration—like it was a badge or something he was wearing.

"A thing happened in Vietnam when I was there. I'm late telling you but I'm doing it now and you can decide afterward if you want me." His voice had gotten stronger, Faye could tell. Once he'd started it was like he was over the hump, and she listened with her head on the pillow, wide-eyed and startled at this turn of things that had to do with him and not with her at all. He was talking about war. He was talking about someplace she couldn't even find on a map.

"It gets hot or sometimes just in the dark I think I'm back there again. Birds calling. That hollow, long sound that seems like the jungle. I never minded too much. It was walking. It was outside. When the mortars got far enough off it was like they were gone. You get used to it. It's like anything else. You can get used to grass roofs and houses stuck on posts in the river."

J. B. let her hand go and Faye listened and she thought he was shrinking away in the darkness. He was quiet. The moon rose outside the window.

"I never saw the things like they say happened there. I never did see any dead babies or girls with their throats cut. Weeks, months maybe and all there'd be was women working in the rice paddies and old men. It's pretty. It's real green. Even with the shelling going it looks like it's supposed to be peaceful. We'd get men blown up with mines and full of shrapnel from grenades or caught in a chopper draft, and it was like the war'd come shrieking in from nowhere. You give a man morphine. You stop him from bleeding to death and you see he's screaming and all you can hear is that noise inside your own head, like the volume's got turned up on something that was there all the time.

"It's a thing you can do, though. You can live with it."

The moon was shining in at the window and Faye could see the faint glint of it in J. B.'s eyes. They were locked on the ceiling. "What I did was leave somebody to die. They came in with the dust-off with fire all around and they grabbed me and took off and he was still flinching there on the ground. You could see him from the air."

His voice still had its steadiness. Faye thought it did, but there was something that had gone out of it that left it sounding flat, even desolate. "What's a dust-off, J. B.?" she said picking at the sheet hem with her finger.

He turned his head and he stared at her a minute and then he looked back at the ceiling. "A chopper coming in to take the wounded," he answered finally, and Faye raised herself up on her elbow.

"Well how come they took you, J. B.? Did you get wounded?"

He had his hands on his chest, and he turned them over back and forth and then he rolled over onto his side with his back to her. Faye put her arm across his waist. "You get wounded, J. B.? I never heard that you did."

She waited. It was like waiting other places in the quiet when you knew something was there.

"I had blood on my forehead. I heard the click and it was like a baseball bat slammed down my whole body and he was sprawled up the path from me. Maybe I blacked out. We were airborne and he was lying there and I was yelling and there wasn't any way to go back in. He was lying there dying."

"But you, J. B. How bad were you hurt?" Faye felt her heart beating faster and she was holding her breath, thinking maybe all this did have something to do with her. Something to do with what J. B. could do in bed.

"A concussion, that's all. Faye, he died out there by himself. He wasn't just anybody. He was a coon hunter from Arkansas and he was as good a friend as I ever had."

"You all right, J. B.?"

"I told you now. You got a right to know. You want a man—you think you could have a man, Faye, that left his best friend to die?" His eyes were shining at her. They were the deer eyes again and Faye knew all at once she had a power she'd never even thought of.

"I guess I don't get it. I don't see it was your fault. It's all right, though, J. B. You're real good to people and me," she said, and they were done talking. The questions were gone, and there was J. B. instead with his slowness and goodness and the damp smell of his hair and the groan of the bed that was his grandmother's, as loud as a shot fired in darkness.

⁓

Her child, when he was born, astonished Faye. He looked like no one. Her father studied him hopefully through the nursery window looking for signs of Faye's mother, but there was no mark of the Nortons' side nor even any suggestion of the broad and dominating forehead of the Davenports. Even less was there a hint of his father, but instead only a healthy, ruddy, and squalling baby boy who could have come from anywhere.

Faye adored him. She did not actually adore him at once. She had awakened from his birth longing to see him, to sort clear of the dreams of anesthesia which had made him half girl and half boy, and puzzling that she was waking up for the first look at a child she had promised herself she would see and feel as it was born. Then she dozed asleep again and in waking, dim flashes remembered the hurried talk and gleaming lights and whisking silence that had carried her away beyond the threshold of long and intense pain.

And the child then, brought to her wrapped like a sausage, tightly, and with nothing of Jamie even in its startled eyes. Faye couldn't understand. She had kept her secret from Jamie with the firm belief that in doing so she would keep the child his—a son in the very image of his father. She had expected that. She had feared it, too, only slightly less than she desired it, and who now could know this baby who seemed neither Davenport or Norton, and not Squires? She named him Timothy and changed his middle name to Sidney from Norton as fast as Glenn Pritchard called him TNT. By the time he was three days old and she took him home, she loved him to a complete and utter distraction.

Her marriage was not something that aroused such clear emotions in Faye. When her child was very young and she lay awake at night waiting for him to cry, she would listen to J. B. breathing as he slept beside her, and she would think about J. B., trying to sort the things she had known about him before they were married from what she had learned since. There was not, it seemed to her, much difference. She thought she had known forever who J. B. was, that his grandparents had raised him, his grandmother keeping to herself and his grandfather fishing all the trout streams and setting traps. Faye had known, too, that J. B.'s grandfather taught him to be a trapper the way he was himself, but that when his grandfather died J. B. had never set a trap again. Faye knew that because people knew it. When J. B.'s number was too high for the draft, he volunteered for the medics and people even said it was all part of the same thing, his not doing any killing that didn't use a fishhook, that J. B. in his own way was like the draft dodgers and the peaceniks had been.

Not that anybody ever really held it against him. He was J. B. after all.

Faye was waiting to hear more. She thought there must be some idea that went with not fighting, with volunteering—something like the Virgin Birth that you believed in or didn't—and she was waiting to see just what it was that J. B. thought. It seemed to her like the kind of thing a man should tell his wife, but all she could come up with was that J. B. had two years in the army and only one war story (which he was done telling after he told her once) and that there wasn't so much an idea he had as just a plain stubbornness about not having any quarrel with anybody. That was the whole thing period, she thought. There wasn't a thing else to it, not an idea at all, and when she'd decided that, it left her feeling disappointed, though in a vague way she couldn't quite put her finger on.

Not that there weren't things she'd found out about J. B. He was as good as could be helping at home and when they took Tim places, he carried him forever like he wasn't even tired. He was crazy about Tim, and he'd play with him on the floor, Tim wiggling on his blanket, and then pick him up and hold him on his chest and never even move when Tim fell asleep. It was like Tim was his. Faye would think that, watching them together, and then she'd wonder if Jamie would've been the same way, and it seemed to her that it was all right thinking of Jamie like that. It was different, somehow, thinking of him for Tim than for herself.

She would lie awake waiting—sorting, tallying—and it seemed to her finally that what was new really wasn't, that as many good things as she could chalk up for J. B., none of them was anything she wouldn't have expected from the way he was before. So maybe he'd gotten his landlady to give them the big apartment on the back instead of the two rooms he used to have and maybe after Tim was born he'd worked overtime, saving money so they could have their own place in town and her father could laugh talking about his daughter with the two houses, if you called a river cabin a house. Maybe J. B. did buy her flowers when they'd never even had a fight, but wasn't every bit of this just being J. B., J. B. like he always had been? It was like a flat-out dead end, hunting for something any different, and Faye gave up as often as not when she was lying there and let her mind drift back slowly to Jamie, being careful, though, that she kept where her thoughts were going tied to Tim.

What she couldn't get over, what she never really had gotten over, was saying good-bye, Jamie charging behind her up the path and then catching up to her with his long strides. He'd taken hold of her but she'd kept trying to run, her sandals skidding on the walk and the lightning bugs flashing in the grass, and then he'd simply turned her around so she was facing him and held her caged so she couldn't move. She stood there, her head down like a sulky child.

"You running away? What are you running from?" he said. He wasn't laughing. He was asking her like he knew everything was wrong, and Faye pushed her forehead up against his chest and then they started walking next to each other but not touching.

"I told you," she said. She was half-whispering and she was trying to keep her voice steady. "Jamie, you got things to do. I'd just as soon be settled and I'm marrying J. B. He asked me."

"J. B. Truman?" Jamie was gaping at her. "*J. B.?*" He was stopped still and Faye looked to see if Hazel's lights had gone on from when he yelled. "What do you mean you're getting married?"

"I just am." Faye looked at him and what she wanted was to hurry. She wanted to be inside the house with the door shut and in her bed with her face in her pillow and the whole thing finished, but she couldn't see leaving Jamie hollering on the front lawn.

"Shhh, quiet," she said. "Hazel and my dad."

"I don't care if your Aunt Lily hears!" Jamie looked wild. He looked like his hair could stand on end, but he'd quieted down some and he followed her around to the back porch. "Faye, you been funny all night. This your idea of a joke?"

He was angry, Faye realized, and she was glad he was. It made it easier somehow. It made her feel tougher inside for what she was doing. "I *am* marrying J. B. It's nothing to do with you," she said, and then she faltered looking at him. There was something skittery, something strange that had just come into his eyes and for a second she thought he knew.

"Oh, Jamie, good-bye," she said. She reached up and kissed him hard and then she ran inside into the dark of the kitchen and upstairs.

She would think all that, feeling shaky, and pretty soon Tim would move, starting his wake-up squeaks, tuning up to cry, and Faye would jump up to get him and feed him before he woke J. B.

When she'd been married long enough that she was used to it all, when she could make J. B.'s lunches without thinking twice about what he'd want on his sandwich and get Tim's car seat buckled while he was still in it, Faye would wonder sometimes that she felt as old as she did for somebody who was only twenty. It was like she was done being a girl, that something in saying her vows or in keeping Tim from falling down the basement stairs had made her as different inside as J. B. seemed the same.

She didn't mind. She didn't think she did. But she'd zip up Tim's snowsuit to take him to her father's, and she'd think about yesterday or the last minute she'd zipped this very same zipper, and she'd sit down on the couch with her hat and coat on staring at Tim trying to chew his mittens off the mitten strap, and she would wonder where she was, who she was, this Faye Truman who'd done in Faith Davenport, and why she felt like the needle on a cracked record that was pawing away forever at the same place.

Going to see her father, though, taking Tim, was something of all the things in her life that she really loved. She loved it absolutely, and Tim loved it so well that she was nearly jealous. She would settle him on the sled and the two of them would go off with the snow falling or the sun shining and Tim and her father would shout greetings at each other and then Tim would stand up high on his grandpa's lap in the window of the truck cab, blaring the horn at her.

It was different, her father said, having a boy to show things to, and when Faye gave Tim his bath at night and he splashed with his cars and airplanes, blowing on the water to make their engines roar, she would smell a stirring, faint scent of grease and rubber in his hair.

He had curls at his temples when his hair was wet, but that was all. His hair had turned black the way her mother's had been and people seeing him with J. B. would say they looked alike, and if a person just looked at their hair it was true they did.

Faye wanted another baby. She wanted one for J. B., to make things fair, and she wanted a girl, but nothing seemed to happen. By the time Tim was four, it occurred to her that maybe J. B. had known all along he wouldn't be a father and that he'd jumped at the chance of having Tim when she'd just thought he wanted her. But none of that squared with anything she knew and anyway it wasn't like him. Faye decided she was getting mean-tempered on top of old and she should make up her mind to have better things to think about people, including J. B. She decided, too, she'd teach him to really swim when they went to the cabin on the weekends and his days off in the summer. She thought he'd like it, that it was something special she could do for him and they could have races back and forth from their dock to the other side.

J. B., though, didn't seem all that interested or maybe he was scared of the river water, of the current, even though where they were was mostly shallow, so instead Faye worked on teaching Tim the dog paddle and the backstroke and how to float and bob up in the water for a breath, while all the time J. B. kept on in his own way, not listening to the ball game, and cooking his fish on a wood fire instead of a grill and Faye didn't really mind but still wondered why he never changed. Sometimes she'd take Tim and Candy Halfacre—Candy Raffin now—and her little girls and go up to the cabin in the afternoons when J. B. was working. She and Candy would race each other across the river and back while Tim and the girls played in the sand and Candy's dog barked to keep the smaller one from getting too close to the water. Then she and Candy would sit on the dock with their feet dangling and watch the girls bury their legs while Tim made tunnels around them, and they'd talk about how long it seemed since they were the girls like the ones you saw at the root beer stand now waiting to talk to the boys.

Faye thought Tim was spoiled or about to be. He had his grandpa buying him miniature license plates from every state in the union and Hazel and Glenn and her Aunt Lily and her Uncle Jeff all acting like Tim was their grandchild, too, though they had their own, and there was J. B., who couldn't see a thing wrong with Tim ever. Faye thought Tim was bold sometimes and she made herself be strict with him when she felt like laughing instead at how smart he was at getting ahead of her and she'd worry over it with Candy and they'd tell each other there was nothing that changed your life like having a child.

They had their birthday parties for their kids together, she and Candy. They'd done it since Tim was one and had a candle as big as his cake, and Candy had brought her brand-new baby girl in an infant seat and set her on the table where she could stare at the balloons hanging from the light. Every year since, Faye had made the cakes for all the parties and Candy got the chips and hot dogs since she got something off her meat with Ted working at the locker.

It was Tim's sixth birthday party that Faye always remembered as the time when everything started to change. Tim had five boys from his kindergarten, but Candy's girls did their share of breaking balloons and getting ice cream on the rug, and Faye cleaned it up and Candy tried to help and then started crying when the crepe paper came down from the ceiling where Faye had taped it. It stuck in Faye's hair and Faye said Candy was crazy, crying over ice cream and crepe paper, but then she saw Candy's face and realized it was more than that. When she'd driven all the boys home and stopped at Hazel's for Tim and the girls to go in and show Glenn Tim's new fire truck since his grandfather was still on the road, she and Candy sat in the front seat with the windshield frosting over, and Faye heard the whole story about Ted and Candy getting a divorce, about the entire long string of Ted's girlfriends Candy had just found out about.

Faye was surprised. She wasn't surprised but she was. She knew the way Ted Raffin was all right, but she'd thought Candy did, too, that Candy understood the way he'd been when she married him and had figured out a way she could live with it.

It was after that day, and after she'd gone through Candy's divorce with her, talking to her on the phone ten times a day and taking the girls for a week when Candy had to get away, that Faye started looking at her own marriage differently. It wasn't that Ted Raffin and J. B. had a bit in common. Faye knew like she knew her own name that J. B. wouldn't run around. Not for anything. But there was this new notion she'd gotten from Candy that you didn't necessarily have to always go along with the way a person was. After seven years of being married, it was a startling idea to Faye. When she thought about it hard, when she thought about it by herself down in the basement hanging up the laundry or lying down for a minute on the couch after Tim went back to school at noon, or even drifting off for a nap, wasn't there something in the love part of Candy's marriage that was like her own? It was nothing like the magazines would say, nothing like J. B. not being good in bed since there was something slow and good in what he did that collapsed her brain and shivered her all over, something that was night and day different from the way she remembered it with Jamie, who had always seemed about to boil over. She had loved Jamie and his warmth and closeness and the way he looked and doing what he wanted, but if you said the truth, those things had really been the whole of the pleasure in it for her. Yet with Jamie it had been plenty, while with J. B. it seemed sometimes like everything in the world he was good about just wasn't enough.

That was the place Faye thought her marriage and Candy's were the same. Ted Raffin ran around and Candy felt destroyed, her love smashed right back on her, and J. B. stayed loyal and good and Faye was torn apart by a love she, too, had no place for, though it didn't seem like it was about Jamie, but something bigger and vaguer than a single person. She was thinking about Jamie a lot, though. She had let herself do it after all this business with Ted and Candy. He would pop right up in her mind and it was nothing to do with Tim or having Tim and she just hadn't fought it. It was like the placemats with American eagles that had always seemed to be there and when her other place-mats were dirty she'd given in and used them once and now she used them all the time.

Not that she ever saw Jamie. She'd seen him maybe three times in seven years and never to talk to, but from a distance. He just wasn't around once he'd started college, and since he'd graduated she heard he was down south, in Louisiana maybe, working on something to do with oil rigs.

She thought she could get over what she was thinking and how she felt, that it was a kind of phase she had to get through like the one with Tim when he was a toddler and always putting everything in his mouth that fit, including the electric plugs. Some days she felt really low and she'd lie on the couch until almost time for Tim to get home and wonder how she'd do it, how she'd live another umpteen years of the same dull on dull life she was set in with J. B. All the driving to the cabin weekends and looking through the window at J. B. fish-ing through a hole in the ice while she played checkers or "Go to the Dump" with Tim in the kitchen and tried to keep the fire from going out. J. B. didn't really even like cards and he'd only played at Klein's once in the Wednesday night game when her father asked him, and though he did take her to eat fish sometimes on Friday night, Faye figured by now if she'd seen one fish she'd seen a river full.

She would lie on the couch feeling strange, dizzy even, and then she'd shake herself and get up and fix Tim's milk and graham crack-ers and make him walk down to Hazel's or her Aunt Lily's with her when he got home just so she could hear some talk while he watched TV. Hazel said she was looking skinny and her Aunt Lily said she was spending too much time listening to Candy Halfacre, and Faye thought they were both right, though she wasn't about to admit it to either one.

And anyway, things were better with Candy. She'd met some-body at Klein's that she'd started going out with and she didn't call so much and Faye thought that what was wrong in her own life might get better, too. And then J. B. came home the week after Christmas and said he was laid off for six weeks, maybe more, and the hospital might be closing down from all the empty beds.

Faye couldn't believe it. It was like the stars and the sun, just that certain J. B. went to work and Tim yelled and waved when he saw the ambulance go by. J. B. told her they'd have to cut back, that he figured he could get work making cabinets, but mostly they'd have to scrape by a little and wait and see.

"I could get a job," Faye said. She said it right off without really thinking, and J. B. shook his head, but as the days went by, the idea kept growing and growing on her until she was completely set on it.

She had two ideas in her head, that she could wear her blue skirt and striped V-neck on the first day of work and that she really had Candy to thank for letting her think she could do something new. Even if it was the closest she and J. B. had ever come to a real argument, with J. B. saying she'd wear herself out working all day at some Kmart for no money when she had Tim to take care of, and even if J. B. had gotten temporary work at the lumberyard and her father kept forcing money on her and Glenn Pritchard started hinting about an inheritance from her mother she was due to get now she was twenty-five, Faye had her mind made up. She was getting a job.

Not that she meant to go to work in any Kmart. She got an interview at the tool and die factory, where Janice Martin, she'd known in high school, had a job as a receptionist. Faye took a test fitting pieces of plastic into a wooden crate, and by mid-January, two weeks before Tim's birthday, she'd started work and the pay was all right and the hours weren't bad.

It was like a whole new life. Faye curled her hair in the mornings and she taught Tim to fix his own lunch and she dropped him off to stay at Hazel's until schooltime. She felt rattled at first, trying to learn what it was she was supposed to do, and she got headaches from all the people talking and the machinery clanging, but by the time she got her first paycheck at the end of the month and then got asked out after work by the people in her section, she was starting to feel like a regular even though she had to say no so she could go on home to get Tim and fix supper.

It was like waking up—she felt that—waking up after a long sleep and finding everything brand new and interesting. She did get tired at work sometimes, and there were times when she'd lie awake half the night worrying about getting enough sleep to be sharp all day, running her machine. She had guilt attacks, too, thinking about Tim coming home to an empty house when Hazel and her Aunt Lily were gone and worrying about him staying at school all day without a break at noon. But J. B. did take him to lunch with him sometimes, and there were the neighbors he could call if anything happened, and Faye told herself besides that it was good for Tim learning about responsibility and independence so early, being an only child like he was.

What she found out she liked best at work was being with all the people. In a way, it was like going to school again, having people notice when she wore something new or did her hair a different way. There were women that called her honey and said she didn't look a day older than their daughters who were eighteen, and in two weeks' time or less she felt like she had a clock inside her telling her it was ten fifteen and break time. She'd sit drinking coffee, and she'd look at people's pictures from the weddings they'd been in or hear what their kids were doing in school, and she'd remember things to tell Tim, funny things like the man from the maintenance crew taking his garbage to the dump and finding a skunk in the can when he opened it.

Faye thought she was good at her job. She'd heard the foreman had gone out of his way to keep her on his shift, and even after she found out he was a friend of Glenn Pritchard and that Glenn had put in a good word for her, Faye still believed him when he said he knew a first-rate worker when he saw one. She was good with her hands. She always had been good with her hands, and she was quick picking up the part of the work that ran off a computer.

She'd tell J. B. about it sometimes after supper when they were doing the dishes. She'd stand scrubbing a pan and she'd try saying just what it was she liked about going someplace where a lot of people counted on her to do a job right, but J. B. didn't say too much and she didn't know if it was because he was laid off again and working in the backroom most days on his cabinets (and *freezing*—she'd told him they should put in a stove or a kerosene heater and she was saving her money to get him one), or because he didn't like it she was gone so much. Maybe there was something else. He said all right, though, when she told him they'd asked her to join the Thursday night bowling team, and she knew he made a point of doing something special with Tim then, even if it was just drawing pictures with new crayons. Sometimes, getting ready to go, zipping up her bowling bag, she thought she'd just gone right around J. B. instead of solving her problem with him in it, that everything had changed too fast instead of in its own time, and she'd worry about that, but mostly she just felt better about herself. She was having fun.

It was bowling where she met Hemp Daniels. She'd seen him before at the plant. He worked out front with the heavy machinery and she'd noticed him sometimes in the parking lot or sitting down at the end table at break time. She spotted him right away because his hair was so red and because he had a voice that sounded like it was coming off the radio. It was funny; it was a round and smooth kind of deep purr.

What he did, she'd noticed, was flirt with the girls, and sometimes even the older women. It was nothing too much, just a comment maybe about how they looked like they were still in a mood to party from the night before. Faye thought he was fresh. She thought he was forward. But he got quieter somehow when she was around. She could tell that he did. It was like he'd noticed something different about her and was different himself. She'd go by on her way back to her machine and he'd be leaning over in his chair talking to somebody and it was like his voice eased off. There was something in it that sounded like he was in two places.

Or maybe it was her imagination. Faye thought she was the last person in the world to guess right about men, somebody like she was that spent her time with people that were grandfathers, or J. B. What did she know about men that weren't married and didn't have kids and looked like they could be in the movies if they didn't have such red hair?

But it wasn't her imagination, was it, when she was bowling on the lane next to Hemp Daniels and he bought her a beer after she got her first strike?

"What's your friend's name, Janice?" he said, and when Faye looked at him with Janice talking, she felt light-headed in a way she hadn't in years.

She talked to herself about it afterward. It was one thing, she knew, to go bowling one night a week for fun, and it was one thing to think about an old boyfriend she was connected to forever whether she liked it or not, due to Tim, but it was something else altogether being a married woman like she was and getting rattled over somebody that looked like he could do the six foot four body-builder ads on TV.

Faye wished she hadn't drunk the beer. She got up early in the morning and fixed J. B. a big lunch, and when he looked surprised she kissed him and said she'd get off at three if she could and pick Tim up at school so they could go to the cabin early for the weekend. She cleaned his fish for him, too, when they went, and she and Tim sat curled up in the chair by the stove while J. B. read to Tim about Sleepy Hollow from one of his grandmother's books.

The next week, though, it wasn't any better. Not only did Hemp Daniels buy her a beer, but he took the chair next to her and started talking to her in between frames about what it was like working on a cattle ranch in Montana. Faye guessed he wanted to impress her, but it didn't really seem like he was bragging since he'd tell a story on himself sometimes, like how he'd branded his boot when he was reaching for a calf. She decided he was just trying to entertain her, trying to be friendly, but she didn't finish her beer. She set her glass down on the table half full and left it there.

It was the beginning anyway. It was actually past the beginning, but what she told herself later, months afterward when it was all over, was how she hadn't given in without a fight. There were weeks that had gone by before she'd ever even said yes to going for a drink with the rest of them after the last frame, and wasn't it weeks more before she'd let Hemp engineer it so the two of them got left together for him to drive her home?

But the truth, she knew, was she had felt what was happening all along. She had known. Why else had she hovered over J. B. so at first? She had had it on the tip of her tongue a hundred times to tell him, *Stop me, J. B. Keep me home. Keep me away from Hemp Daniels and the thousand million others out there just like him.*

Instead she told him once, "There's a Daniels fellow that bought me a beer. He's a big flirt," and J. B. just took it. It was like he noticed and he didn't. It was his same stubborn putting up with things that she might have thought once was Catholic or Christian, except that J. B. missed Mass without a blink when the fishing was good, and so it was just J. B.

Faye was in a fever. Working she was steady, and at home she played marbles with Tim like she always had until they both had holes in their blue jeans from being on their knees, but inside herself she felt on the edge of some delirium, some rocking madness that was not really like being in love, but instead, uncontrollably excited. She was past straight thinking. She knew she should wonder if everything she'd ever heard about Hemp Daniels was true. She did not. Maybe he *had* killed a man in Montana. Maybe he'd lived with a dozen women and left everyone of them the worse for it. Maybe he had ruined as many marriages.

What did any of it have to do with anything? Faye closed her eyes and in a gray wind she was roaring through the air, flying in Hemp's stories. Week after week, the bowling team leaned on Klein's bar or swung their feet against the bar rail, and Faye lived in Hemp's big sky that moved to the horizon and in how he laughed so it sounded like an echo. There was something, too, in the tautness and the suggestiveness of his hands, in the habit he had of making his voice just low enough that only she could hear it.

What it came down to was she wanted him. The sense of it, the power was so intense that it eclipsed all love, all memory so that Jamie, the god to her love, was gone, and J. B., who was there in her eyes in her own kitchen frying her Sunday breakfast, had ceased to have importance.

Yet she waited. On Monday she spent her break studying computer manuals and on Tuesday and Wednesday when a single look at Hemp, walking past her table, would have meant he was standing outside the front gate at closing time, she kept her eyes straight ahead. By Thursday she was sick. At noon she splashed her face with water in the washroom and felt dizzy and wanted to go home. When she'd stayed anyway and then raced through fixing supper and helping Tim with his spelling before Janice picked her up, she didn't know if she was sick or just running way, way past high.

She rolled the best game she ever had. It was like a fast movie with the pins popping up and then smashing away out of sight. The ball thundered on the lane. The pins crashed and Janice gave her a high five and pounded her on the team emblem on her back, and the whole time Hemp was there. He was next to Faye even from across the room.

It was that sense of him, the closeness she knew she couldn't overcome.

And she was calm finally. At Klein's she told Janice she'd catch a ride, and she let the others drift away, one by one, leaving their drained beer glasses and the peanut shells scattered beneath their bar stools. It was just the two of them left, Hemp studying his forehead in the mirror.

"You need a ride home?"

"Yes." Faye had her jacket buttoned, the collar up, and she heard the change clink down beside his glass and felt his hand light at her waist, pushing her toward the door, and she was still calm.

"You all right?"

Faye laughed, and she was like some icy princess being driven through darkness to a fire, and there was Hemp at her ear and no, he knew she wasn't stuck up. He'd only thought so once.

But the fire had come with his hands and mouth. Faye held her breath, and her mind stuck in one place: here she was once more, Faith Davenport, hung up somewhere between love and sex. Here she was in the back seat of a car all over again.

⁓

Had she planned her affair, had she had it in her to plan an affair, Faye did not think she could have engineered a more desirable and, to her, unexpected combination of excitement and pure pleasure. And yet when she wondered over it, as she did in all the time of the affair's two-month meteoric ride, she felt just ordinary. She was not changed by her delight in any way she thought was basic. She had no black chasm in her of guilt, and no sense of herself as wicked or daring. Being with Hemp Daniels was just something she was doing, and it seemed in its way as inevitable to her as her father loving Tim and turning half his basement into a racetrack for Tim's cars. They were alike, somehow, the two things. For all their presumption, neither Hemp nor the track seemed extravagant.

Faye did not think anyone knew. Hazel and her Aunt Lily sniffed around as always like two bloodhounds, but with only their usual complaints about girls with jobs and families who never even had the time of day. Her father was on the road all of April and Glenn Pritchard was laid up with shingles and, if Art Klein gave her a strange look once or twice, it was true, too, that Art made his living by keeping his mouth shut. And who was there to know about her at work with Hemp still flirting full-time with everyone the way he did? No, if anyone would know it was J. B., and he took her excuses of headaches and her sudden plans for shopping trips without seeming a bit suspicious.

It annoyed Faye. She gave herself a little more room, staying later with Hemp at Klein's when the others had left and even letting him phone her at home once. Sometimes she thought her mother knew. She had a vague feeling of someone watching her that was the same as she'd had with Jamie, and for that matter even with J. B. Sometimes she would catch herself up short and *try* to feel guilty. She would close her eyes and see every nun she'd ever known in her whole life ranting about sins against God.

But how, Faye asked herself, could what she was doing be a sin against God before it was a sin against J. B.? And how in all the world could it be a sin against J. B. when he didn't even bother to notice? No, she'd found something extraordinary *and* ordinary in the plain easiness of the right man, in this thing which had defused a part of her that was near explosion, and she knew she'd stick with it as long as it was there.

As though it was hard! Oh, she loved just thinking of Hemp, or a certain thing he did to the ridge of her back that broke her up laughing. He was as funny maybe as he was good looking, and then, too, she had never gotten over his voice. She could float through a whole day at work from just her name buzzed once in her ear at break time. It was like being in a Walkman when Hemp talked, with his voice making stars the whole way around her.

They had Mondays sometimes after work. Some Saturdays she could get away, but Thursday nights were ironclad.

"You're mother'd go bowling if she broke both arms," J. B. said, and Tim looked like he wanted to pout, but he didn't. He was growing up, Faye thought, growing away, and the very idea of it sent a cold chill through her.

Hemp liked Tim. By accident they'd met one day at the pool and, introducing Tim, seeing him with a strange and anxious pride, Faye realized that Tim was funny, too, that he had a disarming way about him that went beyond the family.

But her Thursdays. The bowling leagues were done, and some of the bowlers were stretching out the season with challenge games, with games for the highest straight pin totals. Faye signed up. She got Janice to sign up. She got everyone she knew to sign up. There was a specter before her of the summer and of a week on the river and of every weekend and the spare evenings in between. She marked bowling dates on her calendar up to June and then looked at the blank dates afterward and started feeling dismal.

It was Janice's idea to have one final grand blast for the team—a dinner before bowling, a party at Klein's afterward. Faye knew she was going, but she had mixed feelings anyway. So all right, things were ending and they might as well have a party, but on the other hand, why say things were done at all? Even if there were more days in the week and different excuses so that something as racy and charmed as what she had with Hemp didn't need to be tied to a bowlers' night, still why mark anything finished?

Faye bought a new outfit. She benched her team shirt for a green blouse so soft in color that it made her hair look as blonde as it did in August and then spent forty dollars on pants to match and ripped up the tags so she couldn't return them. She felt giddy and cross all at once. She got dressed three times and burned her wrist on the oven when she was baking pizza for J. B. and Tim to eat, and then she yelled at Tim like it was his fault.

"Sorry, Tim-o," she said, but she wasn't really. She was still cross and she went out the door with a wet rag tied on her wrist when Janice honked.

The dinner made her even more aggravated. Her wrist hurt and she was at one end of the table listening to a hunting story that started with the cocktails and wasn't finished with dessert while Hemp was clear at the other end next to the new secretary from the front office Janice had invited at the last minute, apparently out of pure wicked-ness. Leaning forward, Faye could see them, the girl's fingers working on Hemp's arm like she thought he was a keyboard, and Hemp fiddling with the girl's sweatband, which God only knows why she'd worn to dinner.

"Hemp Daniels broke the mold for flirting," she told Janice, try-ing to sound like she didn't care and then she knocked over her wine glass with the cuff of her blouse, where it was unbuttoned, and had to pour salt on the tablecloth.

Bowling, things were a little better. Faye felt fluid. She'd had just enough to drink that things looked sharper to her, though her score didn't show it, and she thanked herself she was smart enough to let Hemp buy all the beer he wanted to for anybody without having more than one herself. Her foreman was there and he whistled at Faye every time she got a strike and, for that matter, all the fellows from the loading dock were cheering her on and one of them said, "You got green eyes to go with that? Honey, you look terrific."

She'd show Hemp. She thought she had, and then he sat down next to her and pulled her hair and she wanted to sink right back into his shoulder. She wished she could.

The games got ridiculous. Somebody challenged Hemp to bowl a game backward and he did it and almost beat Chip Peacock, who was the long string bean he was rolling against. Faye thought she'd die laughing. She'd lost track of her own score. Her scorecard was covered with blotches and numbers she wasn't sure of, but she kept bowling anyway.

Sometime around eleven, people started leaving for Klein's. Faye waited for Hemp and then when she saw him coming with his car keys in his hand, she ducked off and caught a ride with Janice. She didn't know why. She felt ornery, contrary. She felt a whole list of things she'd learned the names of from her mother.

Klein's was already filling up when she and Janice arrived, and Hemp was there before them, playing pool with Ted Raffin. Ted nodded at Faye.

"You seen Candy around lately?" he said, steadying his cue on the edge of the table, and Faye shook her head and realized it was a week since she'd even thought about Candy, let alone seen her.

"You run into her you can tell her I'm waiting for that money she owes me," Ted said, taking his shot, and Faye didn't answer him. She set her bowling bag down on a table and went up to the bar.

"You drinking, Faye?" Art Klein asked, and Faye told him a root beer and looked in the mirror at the back of Hemp's head and thought for the three hundredth time he was the redheadest man she'd ever seen. She'd gotten so she liked it. His hair was different colors actually and it was sticking out now at the cowlick the way it did when he'd just had it cut. He was a red spot moving around in the mirror, and Faye watched him and looked at the old newspaper jokes crumbling on the wall and the cartoons around the edge of the mirror. Years ago when she'd come here with her father they'd shocked her, these men's jokes, funny and a little raw about saggy old ladies that were topless because their miniskirts couldn't cover what they needed to and bombshell blondes who turned corners in sections, but now they seemed as familiar to her and as nearly an easy part of Klein's as its rows of bottles.

"Your peppermint's empty," she said, looking at Art and pointing to the schnapps bottles on the top shelf, and Art reached down under the counter and got a refill.

"Your dad on the road?" he said, pouring a beer. "I got a truck I'm dealing for I need him and Jeff to look at. Jeff and Lily up at the lake?"

"Maybe," Faye said. There were people on both sides of her she didn't know and she picked up her root beer and got up and walked past Hemp and she knew it was Ted Raffin, not Hemp that tickled her in the ribs. There were kids playing video games and Faye watched a minute and then she put some money in the jukebox. She was thinking of her wedding all at once, of dancing with J. B. ten feet from where she was standing right now and how he fed her lobster afterward, and she suddenly felt so sad her face was quivering, but maybe it was the song, this Kenny Rogers wail that was cranking the tears out of her.

"You going on the bowling tour, Faye?" Chip Peacock said and Faye said what tour and wiped her eyes and perked up a little, thinking there was something happening maybe she didn't know about.

"The pros. You been rolling the ball," Chip said and Faye almost laughed but there was Hemp done shooting pool and Miss Typing Fingers all over him.

"I'll play you a game of pool," Faye said, dumping her change on the table and feeding a quarter into the slot, and Chip skunked her, but she didn't really care.

She was looking for a ride home. She was thinking about walking and then Candy came in and got ambushed into an argument with

Ted by the front door, with him leaning against the wall so she was trapped.

Faye sat down. She was waiting, waiting for two grown people making their fight in public so it was a fire hazard with the door blocked. They were louder than the jukebox and then Ted went on out, banging the door. Candy went up to Art for cigarettes and then looked over at Faye to follow her into the ladies' room.

"You all right?" Faye said, going in after her and closing the door. Candy was splashing water on her face and, when she'd dried it, she got her cigarette package open with her hands shaking and lit a cigarette.

"They need a law," Candy said. "How come they don't want a butcher in Alaska? Faye, you don't know the half of it. Where've you been? I had the phone company see if your line was dead, but then I got J. B."

"No place. Working." Faye pulled a towel out of the dispenser and started rubbing on her nails. "You sound like Hazel," she said, but the fact, she knew, was that Candy got her secrets out of her like Hazel never ever could. "I'm with people," she said.

"Hemp Daniels?"

Faye wadded her towel up and dropped it in the waste can. She nodded. She wasn't going to blush. She wasn't going to get flustered. "Janice and there's Chip Peacock and Hemp Daniels and his new girlfriend from the front office."

"Faye Truman, you think I don't know?" Candy was blowing smoke out of her nose like a bull, and she was shaking all over. "Scratch your best friend even and everybody under the skin turns out like Ted Raffin."

"No." Faye shook her head. "It's not like that. No," she said again, but she didn't know what it really was like and she backed up to the sink and let Candy get by.

"I got the girls in bed," Candy said. "Dumb me needing a smoke. God, he gets me going. Sorry, Faye."

She was gone when Faye went back into the bar. Hemp was playing cards and Faye knew he was drunk. He was arguing with the shift foreman, who was drunk, too, and he kept rubbing his back up against the typing girl who was leaning over his chair.

"I'm going," Faye said. She didn't say it to anybody in particular, but she thought Janice and Hemp could both hear her if they wanted to. Janice was drinking something foamy pink and Faye thought her eyes were starting to cross.

"You leaving already?" Chip Peacock said. "I'll buy you a drink," but Faye shook her head and picked up her bowling bag and then she felt Hemp's fingers on her wrist.

"Ouch. I burned it," she said. He was leaning back in his chair, and she thought he'd tip over.

"What's wrong with you? You on your high horse, stuck up?" he said and maybe he was trying to tease her, Faye thought, but his tongue was just too slowed down to do it.

"See you at work," she said, and then Janice, with her mouth puckered full so she couldn't talk, started pointing toward the door and there was J. B.

"Evening, J. B."

"J. B. Truman."

There were greetings all around the bar, just like he was a regular, and there he was under the clock, which was striking twelve, with his hair combed back and his shirt buttoned up at the collar so he looked like a little boy or somebody who was eighty.

"Where's Tim?" Faye said.

"Sleeping. Your dad's picture tube went. He's watching the late show at our house, so I came over like you said."

"Like I said?" Faye stared at him.

But then maybe she had told J. B. what Janice had said about bringing somebody. "Sure, J. B." Faye shifted her bowling bag to her other hand. "I was ready to go home."

"Who's your friend?" Hemp was getting up from the table, trying to steady himself with his arm. "Hemp Daniels," he said, sticking his hand out at J. B.

"J. B. Truman."

"Her husband?" Hemp was feigning surprise, feigning conscious-ness, Faye thought, watching him weave next to the table. "Any friend of Faye's a husband of mine. Cards?"

"Let's go, J. B.," Faye said. She was ready to say her head hurt, which it did, but J. B. was sitting down in a chair Chip Peacock had pulled up, and Hemp was dealing the cards.

"You sure Tim's asleep? My dad goes to sleep and he won't hear him."

"He's asleep." J. B. had his cards up close to his chest and there was something set in the way he looked, a stubbornness Faye had spot-ted right away, though she figured nobody else could see it. She stood a minute holding her bowling bag, something working in her stomach. Then she pulled a chair up herself and sat down sideways and leaned on the back. The typing girl was leaving. She was going out the door with the fellow from the dock crew who had the pockmarked face, but Faye felt too tired and too disgusted with everything she could think of to feel glad.

"You're all right, J. B. You get us another pitcher, Art?" Hemp said and Faye watched the cards going around the table again. She didn't know Hemp like this. She didn't know if she could trust him or not and who was J. B., anyway, showing up here at midnight?

"You want some Fritos, J. B.?" she said.

J. B. nodded and pulled at his beard, and Faye went up and reached over the bar and took two bags down from the hook and left her money for Art.

"So what's the movie?" she said.

"I don't know." J. B. had his shirt collar open now, but Faye knew it was from heat, not style. She saw him squinting at his cards and then Hemp was staring at her and maybe he wasn't as drunk as she thought he was. She bit down on a Frito.

"You in, Faye?" he said.

"No."

"I thought you were in."

"Just you men," Faye said, and she stood up. She was feeling edgy, uncertain, and she did something with the zipper on her bowling bag and then got Janice some coffee from the back room and walked her up and down by the bar. She could hear the coins clinking down on the table, and the smoke from Chip Peacock's cigar was making her nose itch.

"Your clock right, Art?" she said. There were only three people left at the bar and he was cleaning up, emptying ashtrays and washing glasses. Faye set her watch for 12:23 and caught Janice before she toppled over onto a bar stool.

"I got work tomorrow, J. B.," she said. "I could drive Janice home if you came after me with the truck."

"He's winning, Faye. He can't leave," Chip said, and Faye wanted to argue, but there was something she felt, some menace in Hemp and the stubbornness in J. B. that kept her from doing it.

"I'll take a beer," J. B. said. He was pink around the eyes. He was pink from the heat or from the game and Faye thought he looked worn out, that the lines looked cut in around his eyes.

"You could play us some music," he said, looking at her with his smile that was a little tired, but still sweet and all J. B. He was pushing quarters at her out of his pile.

"Sure." Faye nodded, but she felt slow. She felt stupid somehow. She walked over to the jukebox and maybe she had the numbers all right and the record was going down, but what in the world was she doing here? It was like she was playing some freakish role. She was Ingrid Bergman with two men and a secret to keep and a bar, and she was doing it with spots on her new pants and a feeling inside her like she'd chewed on nails.

Let's go. Let's go home, J. B.

But she was saying it to herself, bent over the jukebox with its lights flashing.

"You find those queens in your hand?"

"Sure."

"That J. B. stand for jackass bastard?"

"Let's go, J. B!" Faye was back at the table in an instant, pulling on J. B.'s arm, and Hemp was glowering at him and starting to stand up. "You think this is some TV show, Hemp?" she said. "Some Wild West?" She was tugging on J. B., but he wouldn't move. "Hemp, he wouldn't cheat. Not J. B. Not for anything."

"He can take his money. You got your cheater's money, Truman. We'll play for her." Hemp was standing up, pointing at Faye. "She's my stakes. You like that, jackass bastard?"

"We're going, J. B.!" Faye was begging. She was pleading for all she was worth, but J. B. was sitting there like he hadn't understood except to deal the cards.

"This is crazy. Hemp, you're drunk," she said, but it was like she wasn't there. It was the two of them locked head-on in a poker game when J. B. didn't even like cards, and there was Janice staring at them glassy-eyed and Chip Peacock looking like he'd got stuck in some kind of machinery press that was coming at him from two sides.

"You know what he *said*, J. B.? You're not playing for me. I'm not some sack of potatoes you're playing for." Faye was standing over him, but J. B. was looking at his cards, not her, and it was like he was eating a ham sandwich, like it was that important.

"I can beat that pair," he said. He had his queens again, three of them this time, and Faye looked over at Hemp and at the same minute Hemp stood up and knocked everything, the beer pitcher and the glasses and Chip's ashtray and all of the money and cards, onto the floor.

"Get your cheater's money. We can finish this outside," he said.

"You bet you can finish outside. OUT! You get out!" Art Klein was yelling from behind the bar and he had the phone picked up.

"He won't fight, Hemp." Faye was choking, and she didn't know if she was just scared or going crazy or what.

Chip Peacock had Janice by her shoulders and he was half carrying her toward the door and Hemp was looking like an iron man, heated red, and there—Faye couldn't believe it—she *didn't* believe it—there was J. B. on his hands and knees in the beer puddle picking up coins.

"*J. B.!*" She was pounding on his back. "*J. B.!*" She was screaming. What was he doing, a man that took everything like he thought he was a saint or something and she was supposed to live with it? No. She wasn't anymore. The thing that had kept grinding against itself for the whole of her marriage had pulled loose.

"You *fight* him!" Faye was hitting J. B., the back of her fists banging his shoulders like she was playing a drum. "You're a coward, J. B. You're for sure not a man. You're a man that's got no children."

And even that. He slowed down maybe, but he was still picking up coins, and Faye thought she would drown in her own throat. She was crying and she was kicking at the coins with her feet and Art Klein had his hand clamped over her arms. "A coward, J. B!" Faye was leaning over him, over the back of his head. "J. B., you're a man that left his best friend to die."

Where it came from she didn't know. She knew and she didn't know, but it stopped everything in the world and J. B., as if she had taken cold aim and fired. There was a motion like a snake quiver in his spine when he stood up.

"I didn't mean that," Faye said, her voice slipping away, but J. B. had pushed past her, his eyes like they'd left his face, and he was going outside. He was fighting Hemp and she had done it. She had caused it. She had reached to the deep place where he wasn't J. B.

There were headlights on in the parking lot. For a second going out the door, Faye was blinded, but there was Hemp then, stripped to the waist, the lights turning the hair on his chest gold instead of red.

It was like smoke, the light from the cars. J. B. looked skinny, or maybe he just looked pale. His pants were hitched too low, and there was a rash on his neck above his collar, and when he put his fists up Faye was suddenly terrified. He had an idea how to fight. He had an idea the way she did, but there was Hemp with his big shoulders and his stomach that looked like somebody had stitched it flat.

"Hemp, don't hurt him," Faye said. Maybe she was praying. She had her face pushed into Chip Peacock's arm, and Hemp and J. B. were circling in the light beams, J. B. with his eyes half shut. He was making some sound. She thought it was J. B. He was humming something.

Or was it a June bug? There was something flying at Hemp's head and he swatted at it. He swatted again, and J. B. hit him hard in the jaw. Faye could hear the sound of it and then suddenly J. B. was on the sidewalk on all fours from Hemp landing a punch. There was blood on his shirt and shining on his beard and Faye knew he wasn't fighting anymore. He was waiting for whatever else Hemp threw.

"Get up. J. B., get up!" she yelled, but Hemp was on him. It was like a wrestling match all at once with Hemp pinning J. B.'s arms, jamming his head into the pavement, and then a pop flash of light, an exploding shot and Art Klein was waving his pistol in the air from the warning shot he'd fired and the horn was honking in Chip Peacock's car where Janice had passed out over the steering wheel.

"Get her in the back seat. Move it, Peacock. The sheriff's coming." Art had Hemp up against the front window and Faye wanted to touch J. B. and the smell of his hair that was like asphalt and black things. She was babbling at him, trying to soak up the blood from his face with Hemp's shirt.

———

In her kitchen, Faye thought it was ninety degrees. She was in her shorts talking to Hazel on the telephone, checking on Tim. "It's a steam bath here, too." She was leaning into a cabinet door, the phone cradled under her chin. "Sure it's all right if he stays but none of those movies. Tell Glenn." Faye hung up the phone and got her purse from the counter. In spite of herself, she'd let the time get away from her. She had clothes to pick up at the dry cleaner's and it was almost five.

In her car driving to town, even with the windows open and the vent fan on high, Faye was boiling hot. Two blocks from the dry cleaner's she thought she'd never make it in time. A block away, with a picture in her head of J. B. hugging Tim with his cast to tease him, she remembered all at once that she already had her clothes, that she'd picked them up on Thursday on her way home from work.

Faye slowed the car down and pulled it over to the curb and stopped. She pounded a fist on the steering wheel. So what if J. B. had been the same with Tim the day he got out of the hospital? Why was she even thinking about that? And how in the world had she forgotten she'd already been to the cleaners? It was like her mind had these ruts she kept sinking into and couldn't escape.

Faye pushed her hair up off her neck. She was waiting for a break in the traffic, watching the beer glass on the bar and grill sign fill up. There were lights burned out in the glass outline and she wished the beer would just pour down onto the street in a big neon flood. Finally the last car went by. Checking over her shoulder, Faye pulled out from the curb and made a U-turn.

She was going home, but she was in no hurry. If she could drive away from the heat she'd hurry, but what was the point of rushing home to a house that was hot and empty besides? She could go to Hazel's, and she might as well with a whole Saturday night ahead of her with nothing to do.

Faye turned the corner toward the river, going west. By the time she got as far as Klein's she'd changed her mind again. She wasn't up to Hazel—she couldn't stand the thought of Hazel—but she needed eggs and she thought she might as well get fresh ones. She pulled her car in under the Klein's sign between two pickups and got out, hoping Sue was inside tending bar instead of Art. It wasn't exactly that Art wasn't talking to her. His name had been on the card they'd sent her for J. B., but it still didn't mean he was friendly.

Somebody she didn't know was behind the bar, some substitute from someplace, and Faye thought maybe her luck was changing. There were fans going and she stood in front of the dairy case and felt the dampness on the back of her legs from the car seat go dry. She took her eggs out and went up to the bar and sat down halfway on one of the stools waiting to pay. The jukebox was playing. There was sunlight glinting off the mirror and Faye squeezed the egg carton in her fingers so it squeaked and then looked down the bar into a sunbeam and straight at Jamie Squires.

Faye blinked. It was Jamie all right. He was smiling. He was grinning at her, and wasn't it unbelievably Jamie with the same curly hair and browned face and only his jaw a little wider and his shoulders? He was coming over to her, his glass in his hand, and Faye sat down all the way on the stool and put her eggs down on the counter.

"Jamie," she said. She thought she was smiling and she let him kiss her and she thought, too, that her heart would race, that it should race, that it was racing, but mostly all she felt was a strange sort of emptiness inside her.

"How've you been?" They said it together and both of them laughed. Faye looked at her egg carton and wondered what in the world of all the things she'd said in her mind to Jamie she could say to him in person.

She looked at him. "How long you been home?"

He sat down on the stool next to her. "Since yesterday. You want a root beer?" He was grinning at her with his eyes, which were the same pale and dazzling blue, and he was Jamie for sure but somebody older besides, with a man's look and sound about him. "You still drinking root beer?"

"Sure." Faye wanted to grin back at him, but there was the same dullness inside her. She folded her hands over the egg carton and watched the bartender put her napkin and root beer down with one hand and give Jamie his change with the other.

"So how's your dad?"

"Good. Your folks?"

"Henry's got a gimpy leg is all."

"Somebody said you're working in an oilfield."

"Off shore. The Gulf down south of Baton Rouge."

"Well where's your accent?"

Jamie was drinking his beer, his eyes on her. "You been all right, Faye? I heard you and J. B. split up."

Faye looked at him. She looked at him and she didn't look. She was staring at some spot on his shoulder. "Sort of. He got hurt, but he's all right now."

"Still working on the ambulance crew?"

"He got laid off. He's making cabinets. He was." Faye pushed a hole in the wet spot in the napkin under her root beer. The news was on, and it blared from the television until finally somebody turned it down.

"It sure doesn't change much here." Jamie was looking around. He was looking at the shiny spots on the chairs where the paint was gone and at the clippings on the mirror and maybe he was looking someplace else—at the river and the town and the whole end of the summer out there beyond the windows. Faye pushed her thumb into the catch on the egg carton.

"You believe I tripped on that same hole over there in the linoleum at my wedding dance?" She put her hand on her collar. She was leaning a little inside herself, hearing the music and even remembering the scent of her wedding dress when she pulled it on.

"Sure you did. Who wouldn't?" Jamie answered, and there was something quiet and vacant in his voice, something, Faye thought, of all the silence of the years that had slipped by.

"I got a boy. Tim." Faye turned her glass on the napkin. "He's real smart. He's a lot smarter than me. He knows trucks like his grandpa. He's got a gerbil. He's got a stuffed fish on his wall he caught with his father, and he's just like him, too. He's got his hair. He smiles like him. He fishes like him. He's J. B., Jamie, right down to his toes. So what's it like down there by Baton Rouge?"

"You ever had Cajun cooking, Faye? You got a boy? A water girl like you are, you'd like the bayous."

"Would I? Are they green?"

"They are."

"Oh." Faye was smiling. She felt calm. She felt the way she had when Tim was a baby and went to sleep in her arms in the sunshine, and she could see Tim now, floating in a pole boat on a bayou with his stuffed fish.

"A green place," she said, letting it go. She was still smiling, drifting off from the place in her head that was green once, too, the place where she'd kept them all a family.

"Well it can't be hotter than here," she said, standing up. She had her egg carton. "It's real good to see you, Jamie."

"You going? How about dinner? I could fix you those eggs." He was feeling his way. Faye could tell he was, but she shook her head.

"No. I'm going someplace," she said. She leaned over him, Jamie this beautiful boy still, and kissed him next to the ear. "Thanks for the root beer," she said.

And she *was* going someplace. She was going to the cabin to find J. B., and if it was true she didn't feel any better than she had in ages, or at least in the last two months, she did feel certain. She looked back at Jamie once on her way to the door, and then went on out and started her car.

On the road, the whole long desolation of where she'd put herself moved over Faye like a giant hanging cloud. Maybe a hundred times, maybe a thousand times when J. B. was in the hospital, she'd told herself what the doctors had said about him being all right, and then finally when the swelling in his face had started to go down and he began to eat a little and to say a few words, she had realized that even if he was going to be all right, even if he was perfect, it was plain as could be that the two of them just wouldn't be all right together.

The heat blew over Faye. There were heat waves rising from the highway.

In the hospital J. B. had had nothing to do with her. His eyes wouldn't follow her in the room. He wouldn't speak to her unless he had to. Every day and night when she'd hardly ever been farther away from his bedside chair than the Coke machine in the lounge across from his room, it was like he didn't see her.

She knew she deserved it. She brought Tim to the hospital to visit and asked Hazel to drive to the cabin for books and then she read to J. B. until her voice quit. She got her leave extended from work and she even got so the welts on J. B.'s face looked as normal to her as his beard, but when she took him home finally with everything ready—the house immaculate and flowers and clean sheets in the bedroom and the fan blowing so he could lie down right away if he was tired—it didn't really surprise her that he started putting things in the pickup to go to the cabin by himself.

"You're not strong enough," she said. She was trying not to cry, watching him limp back and forth to take his tools, his clothes.

"I'm all right." He looked at her, his shirt collar buttoned even in the heat, the sleeve flapping open for his cast. There was all the gauntness in him of illness, a white cleanness about him. "We'll talk about Tim later," he said, and then he had driven away.

Faye reached for the radio through a mist of heat, a hot steam in her eyes. She was almost there. She turned off on the road to the cabin and drove through the trees, the radio buzzing with the motor. There was sunlight falling in pinpoints on the fenders.

At the cabin Faye turned the car off and got out and went around the pickup, which was parked by the front porch. One of J. B.'s old shirts was lying on a wheel cover in the box, and she remembered the pocket needed sewing. She stood a minute, listening for the river, and then she went on up the steps.

"J. B." Faye knocked on the screen door. "J. B.?" she called, and she was thinking of what she could say to start with, to break the ice, of all the things she could ask him about like which fuse it was for the garage and who she could call about the wood and about the drip under the kitchen sink and whether Tim should play soccer or flag football when they started and if it was all right for her dad to use the leftover paint for his shutters, but it was quiet inside the house. There wasn't any answer.

"J. B.?" she said one more time and then she went down to the end of the porch and under the railing and headed down the hill to the river.

The canoe was gone. Faye could see a rowboat with a red side way, way downstream, but there wasn't any sign of J. B. She poked around in the weeds a little, looking for Tim's dump truck, but all she found was an old shovel with a broken handle and she left it there and went back up to the house.

"You sure you're not here, J. B.?" She stuck her head in the door, but it was still quiet and she went on in and J. B. had it so clean it surprised her. In the big room the only thing out was a book open next to a candle on the table, like J. B. thought he was Abe Lincoln or something, and in the kitchen there were just two pans and a few dishes in the sink and not much of a ring and Faye had things washed up in a minute and the dish towel drying on the bush outside the window.

She looked in Tim's room, Tim's closet really, since J. B. had built a bed into the wall and a couple of drawers where his grandmother used to keep her brooms. Tim's red shorts were hanging on the bedpost and Faye turned them right side out and put them with her purse. She was missing her cutoffs, and she went to look in the drawers in the bedroom and it was all neat there, too, if you didn't count the bed not being made. J. B. had his jeans on the chair and Tim's school picture was stuck in the mirror and there was a picture of her next to it that Glenn Pritchard had taken when Tim was a baby.

It startled Faye, finding herself there. She hadn't even thought J. B. wanted to look at her and here he had her picture up. But there was another picture, too, a picture she'd come across maybe once before of J. B. in a medic's uniform with his army unit, and seeing it, trying to think which person it was that was his friend, Faye felt the little bit of hope that had begun to glimmer in her die.

She started rummaging through the drawers, all the time trying ideas in her mind, phrases she could say to J. B. about their starting in the wrong place and Tim crying himself to sleep and how she'd made the whole disastrous mess by doing everything she thought she had to one step at a time. She was hunting for her cutoffs and anything like Tim's socks that might turn up, and she'd just knocked the drawer handle that was loose off onto the floor when the light changed in the doorway and she looked up and there was J. B.

"Oh," she said, stepping backward, almost tripping, and it was like she was some guilty burglar caught in the act, even with her own cutoffs in her hand. "I was waiting for you," she said quickly, and maybe he was thinner. His face looked tired and sunburned behind the welts, and with his cast off, his arm had a crinkled, gray look to it like the skin was loose.

"Where's Tim?"

"At Hazel's." Faye tried looking J. B. in the eye, but she couldn't. The drawer handle was under the dresser, and she stooped down and picked it up and put it carefully on the dresser. "J. B., we have to talk," she said, "we haven't talked yet," and she thought she was dressed all wrong, that whatever it was they had to say to each other it shouldn't be with her in her shorts she'd cleaned the house in and a shirt that was all damp with perspiration. And, anyway, why did it have to show so in his eyes what she'd done? She thought she'd break up in little pieces just looking at him.

"You eaten yet? I got some fresh eggs," she said. She followed him out and leaned on the kitchen door and watched him clean his fish. "You got champagne for that? We could say it's lobster and then have champagne." Faye pushed her forehead against the doorframe, and the whole middle of her, up and down, felt like it was stuck with needles. "Tim's real excited about school starting. They got a new fort on the playground he found out about and he can't wait. You want me to go, J. B.? I guess you can just work on that fish and never say a word. Oh, J. B., can't I undo it? Can't I take it all back somehow?"

She had her fists tightened up against the doorframe, and she heard J. B. coming toward her. She could smell the fish and all she wanted for her whole life was to have his arms around her, to feel him holding her so she was wrapped up, but he had her hand instead. He was taking her to the door and he was throwing her out. She thought he was, but he was on the porch instead, bent from the waist against the railing, and finally he let her hand go.

"It's just over, Faye." It was the piano voice, the deep one, the voice to dance to for the slowest dance there was.

"J. B.," she said. "J. B. I never meant to hurt you. If you could forgive me. I saw Jamie Squires and it was nothing, and Hemp Daniels can go rot in some jail or wherever he is. Maybe it took awhile to know it, but I do now. I know how good you are. Tim loves you. And I do. I want us, J. B."

He was shaking his head, a slow and insistent rhythm back and forth, and he turned toward her, and it was his deer eyes again, the fathomless darkness where he loved her.

"No, Faye." He had his head pushed back on his neck somehow. "It was enough having you. I didn't really expect any more. The fight, though . . . the reason for it . . ." J. B. looked off toward the river, and Faye thought he was searching for his dead friend or maybe for himself, for who he was before he knew he hadn't saved his friend. Maybe he was even searching for himself before he understood he hadn't saved her.

He looked back from the river. "It's nothing like forgiving you," he said then. "It's forgiving me. It's like a fish, Faye. He gets hooked in some places and he just lays on the bottom till he's better and then he comes back. He gets hooked someplace else, and even if he gets away, you don't see him anymore."

His face was closed down. It was shut tight against them, and Faye backed off.

She had her purse. She had Tim's shorts and her cutoffs, and there was her car waiting for her out beyond the pickup.

The Battle

I n the summer of big storms—of rampaging, straight-line winds that scattered barn shingles and pieces of metal siding all over the county—Quentin Hinterson's barn blew apart in stages. In the first storm, one with the force of a mild hurricane, the foundation buckled in the southwest corner. A week later, a fierce lashing of rain dumped six inches of water into the rain gauge and caused the creek to skip a bend in its channel, and the barn roof stopped being a roof, springing so many leaks that the hay under it swelled a foot closer to the rafters.

Then the pace of things picked up. One wind hurled a thirty-foot oak branch through the back of the cattle bunker, another ripped off half the shingles, board first, and a renegade glancing twister pulled the siding loose along the whole eastern wall and hurled the scaffolding that had been put up into the pasture. When the big storm hit, flattening trees like so many cornstalks, the barn exploded and fell in a heap as if a bomb had landed square in the belly of it, and Quentin's battle with the pigeons started.

He had been eyeing them suspiciously since the first storm. They were riled up even then, flying in an eerie, silent rush at the nests that had smashed down from the rafters. Now in the early morning they were calling as they flew. They dove in quick, tilting circles in the dead space where the barn had been and Quentin, listening from the porch, watched to see where they would go, but they kept on in place, revolving like satellites to an invisible center.

They were still flying when he finished his morning chores. He had shored up the end of the lean-to in the pasture and strung a charged fence around the barn wreckage to keep his heifers out, and the pigeons were still wheeling and crying in the sky.

"Goddamn noisy place," Quentin muttered. The fencer was clicking and the cattle were bawling in the trees.

At noon, when Quentin had eaten and had gone out to smoke on the front steps, if anything there were more pigeons flying than there had been before.

"A wake," he said. He tightened his eyes and knocked his pipe out on the heel of his boot.

At two o'clock, Quentin looked out the kitchen window at a sky that was thick and dark with swirling pigeons, and at four o'clock he took his gun outside and scattered shots where the barn peak had been. A half an hour later, the pigeons were still flying in full force.

"I can't see why you're so set off by a few pigeons," his cousin said. It was Wednesday, her day to housekeep for him, and she'd come out of the house, a feather duster under one arm and her purse on the other. "Your barn being gone—now that's bad, but pigeons?" She opened her car door. "Quentin, there were socks in the bathtub. You know I hate that."

In the morning, Quentin found the pigeons perched in clumps around the rubble of the barn. He advanced on them from the house, stick in hand, but before he had gone halfway across the yard, they rose into the sky in a long, sweeping line. "You were napping," he yelled, waving the stick, and the pigeons' scream came back to him, a wail that was half bubble, half coo, but harsher than either.

By afternoon Quentin decided he needed help. "Come on, Gopher, get out from there," he said poking under the porch, and his dog, an old collie with a cataract in one eye, bellied out through the dirt and forced himself slowly upright.

"You got any work left in you? Can you herd pigeons? Come on," Quentin said, but the dog just stood looking at him through one eye and then turned around and squeezed himself back under the porch.

"I can get the neighbors' dogs." Quentin kicked at the dirt, and the dog thumped his tail once and then lay still.

"And I pay for you to eat," Quentin said, but he had already given up the one idea and started on the other. "I'll use Sam Taft's hunting dogs," he said, making one last kick at the dirt. He went inside to the telephone.

In an hour the truck arrived with the dogs in it. They were yapping and howling in the back end, and Quentin's dog started a low moaning from under the porch.

"Quentin, I never heard of using hounds on pigeons," Sam Taft said.

"You never had two hundred pigeons pining in your barnyard."

"What I'd do is bulldoze the barn under. Those pigeons'll go."

"I don't want pigeons in the machinery. Or in my oats."

"These dogs need the scent."

"I got a barnyard full of scent." Quentin leaned over, scooping up feathers. "Smell these," he said, pushing them under the dogs' noses while they sniffed and backed, Sam squeezing their leashes. Then all at once they threw their heads up and started caterwauling into the sky.

"They've got it." Sam was laughing and he eased his grip on the leashes. "They've got the scent and they've got your pigeons spotted. What'd you have in mind, Quentin?" The dogs were barking and lunging, and the air was shrill with the noise of pigeons.

"I had it in mind with these dogs we could drive the whole flock across the road to Ez Raffin's field barn."

"These dogs aren't going anywhere. Not as long as those birds are circling." Sam was still laughing. "Quentin, those pigeons are treed."

In the night Quentin awoke from a dream with a sudden determination to get scientific in the matter of the pigeons. He had been dreaming about his wife, a vague, erratic woman whose face had disappeared from his memory in the years since her death, and with the spectral presence of a woman of uncertain features but an unmistakable yellow dress still lingering over him, he made up his mind to be more observant, more clearheaded in his assault upon the pigeons.

The next morning, when he'd finished his chores, Quentin lumbered up the steps of the granary to the loft and stationed himself at the window where he could watch the pigeons without the racket. Through the loft window, they were a hundred yards away but dead ahead, flying at the level of Quentin's eyes.

"Don't you ever get tired?" he muttered, lifting a foot onto a crosspiece that was nailed up between two studs just above the floor. He was out of breath from climbing the stairs and he leaned his shoulder against the wall, trying to get the stitch out of his chest.

"So you get thirsty." A handful of pigeons had peeled off from the main body of circling birds and had swept from the sky to the creek bank. Then they flew back up the hill and, with a slight hitch in motion that was like a shopper's pause at a revolving door, they resumed their place turning in the air above the barnyard. Ten minutes later another batch went down to the creek and in intervals after that, which Quentin timed with his watch at ten to thirteen minutes apart, the rest of the pigeons took turns getting water. But, aside from an occasional bird lighting for a moment on the rubble, they kept on flying. The heifers moved from one end of the pasture to the other, grazing, and Quentin's stomach was growling and empty and the pigeons, their wings hunched back, still flew above the barnyard.

"You pigeons are hungry," Quentin yelled, dragging his foot down from the crosspiece. He rubbed a blue circle on the windowpane where it was fogged with the smoke from his pipe. "You need to eat," he said, stomping his foot on the floor and trying to get the blood circulating through his leg again. Then he lifted his cap and rubbed his hand across his scalp. "I can track greens and mash out past the road. I leave a heap in the barn there, that'll get you." Quentin's eyes ran along the front wall of the granary, and he stiff-legged his way across the floor to the far window. He looked out to Ez Raffin's barn that was standing by itself in the field beyond the road. He stroked his chin. "Well, it'll take some feed," he said.

By the time he had gotten his own meal and had climbed back up the steps to the loft, Quentin had lost his enthusiasm for a feeding plan. "It'll cost too much," he'd told himself in the kitchen with a piece of cold beef pie in his mouth. "They won't eat it if it's got my scent," he decided while he was washing out his bowl. "And who says it'll work?" he asked himself when he passed the barn. "If I start with feed in that rubble, they'll be glad to stay right there."

Quentin took a pencil stub out of his pocket and scratched a line on the loft floor. "No guns," he wrote on one side. "No stick, no hounds, and no feed." He looked at the words and then, putting the pencil away, he went back to his pigeon watch.

It was the heifers who gave him the idea he stuck with. "What are you doing, you whiteface?" he yelled, looking past the barn rubble at a heifer who was forcing her way through a broken fence wire next to the lean-to. "You think you're the head cow—you'll be hamburger!" Quentin clattered down the loft steps and out the door. His pickup was parked in front of the machine shed, and he got into it, racing the engine as he started out across the field, but a whole line of heifers was following the whiteface out of the pasture and it was an hour before Quentin had them rounded up—eating hay in the lean-to—and the fence mended.

"Now think about it," Quentin said that night, dealing pinochle cards to Lloyd Thomas. "A herd has a head cow. Every herd I ever had did. So if you've got a head cow why not a head pigeon? I saw him, Lloyd."

"If you say so, Quentin." Lloyd was sucking on a piece of hard candy and he grinned at Quentin with his tongue stuck in the hole where his eyetooth should have been. "You giving me the queen of spades this time?"

"They go down to the creek in shifts. He's the one that gives the signal. He dips his wings. It's like a fighter plane on TV. Off they go like a squadron. I saw it. I saw him. He's dark gray on top and purple underneath."

"Sure, Quentin." Lloyd picked up his cards, still sucking at the candy and grinning, and Quentin frowned across the table at him. He could forgive Lloyd anything. Lloyd Thomas had lost one son in the jungle war Quentin's own son wouldn't go to, and the very same fall his other son got run over by his own tractor in his own field.

Still, Quentin didn't like being laughed at. "I'll show you, Lloyd," he said. "You come down here tomorrow and we'll flush that head pigeon so he leads the whole bunch over to Ez Raffin's field barn."

"All right," Lloyd said. "But give me ten points for that dix."

It was cool and gray in the morning when he arrived. Quentin was finishing his chores. "I've got the dog in the pickup. We using dogs?" Lloyd asked, and Quentin latched the gate of the chicken coop and dumped an empty feed bag onto the rubbish pile next to the fence.

"Maybe. If Gopher wakes up long enough."

"Come on, Ginny." Lloyd opened the door of his truck and a long, purple Irish setter bounded off the seat to the ground and almost knocked him over. "Calm down. Down, girl," Lloyd said, and he knotted his fingers around the dog's collar and held on while the dog sniffed and rooted up and down the driveway.

"Well, you got Gopher now," Quentin said. His dog had come out from under the porch and was walking toward them. "Let her go, Lloyd," he said, and the two men stood watching while Gopher planted his feet in the gravel and squinted his eyes closed and let the younger dog climb all over his neck.

"You get the cornerstone out?" Lloyd turned toward the barn-yard and while Quentin's eyes fixed on the sky and on the pigeons, Lloyd searched the rubble with his. Then he climbed over a chunk of mortared stone. "Right here, Quentin. Under the beam. Lord, these barns are older than us. 1910. I don't like it they come down."

"I'll get a pole barn up and it won't rot. There he is. See him? He's the fat one shaking his wings."

"How're we going to do this, Quentin?"

"We cut him out of the flock and get him started. Treat him like a cow."

"He's twenty feet up in the air."

"He's suspicious. Look at him quiver. Stare at us, you fat thing!" Quentin had crossed the barnyard, and he was climbing over boards and hay bales, his breath coming fast.

"Bring the dogs up, Lloyd. Easy. He's slowing down. Hold your dog on that rafter."

Quentin felt Gopher nudging at his ankles. "You got the bug, old boy? Look at that pigeon. He gets much slower eyeing us and he falls right out of the sky. By God, she's got him started. That dog of yours has him turned, Lloyd. Give her her head." Quentin was flapping his arms at the whole world of pigeons that was screeching around his ears and, as he scrambled off the board he was balanced on, he felt the mud of the barnyard squish up around his boots and Gopher shoot past him. "That's it! Chase him, boy. Keep the son of a gun going."

They were all running, Ginny leaping and Gopher pounding across the earth, and Quentin's heart felt as big as his chest. "We've got it, Lloyd," he yelled. They were thudding across the ruts of the hay field, and the sky above them was strung now like a longbow with an infinite line of migrant pigeons. They were running, the dogs barking, the pigeons soaring in a flash of wings overhead.

At the ditch along the road, Quentin stopped, his heart roaring. "Here, Gopher," he called. He felt a wet muzzle push into his hand and he crouched down on one knee and circled his arms around Gopher's heaving sides. "Hold on to your dog, Lloyd. See him? He's checking it out to pass at the roof. I knew it! Look at him, Lloyd." Quentin wiped the sweat off his forehead and ran his hand down Gopher's flank.

Lloyd let out a whistle. The pigeons were banking, making a slow, turning arc in the sky, approaching the barn from the north and west and dropping one by one to the peak, to the shingles of the roof.

"That's him landed first, plumping his feathers." Quentin's tone was hushed, but his voice was shaking with excitement. "I told you, Lloyd."

"So that's a head pigeon." Lloyd had his hand on Ginny's collar. "Quentin, this is fun. I haven't had fun like this since I was hunting with my boys."

"Sure," Quentin said. For an instant, for a flash of time, he thought of his own son he'd heard from once in a letter he'd burned in the stove. He set his lips in a thin line and then, pushing on Gopher, he raised himself upright.

"We got trouble, Lloyd. Look at him."

"Is that him calling?

"There's something bothering him." The pigeon had left the peak of the roof and was flying back and forth beside the barn.

"He'll take the whole bunch back."

"No he won't." Quentin had cleared the ditch and the fence and he was headed across the road to the barn. "Get on back, you. Shoo." He shook his fist at the pigeon and from the corner of his eye saw the agitated flap of wings of the other pigeons on the roof. "You're not taking them back."

The pigeon was diving now and Quentin saw the dip of his wings, the signal. "I'll show you, bird."

Quentin dug in the grass beside the barn, scrabbling, and he had found the stone he wanted. He wrenched it from the ground. "You're not going anywhere," he screamed. He could feel the bulk of the stone in his fingers, the sharp point of it pressing in the center of his palm. His weight was even on his feet. He drew his arm up, cocking it behind his head, and with his eyes narrowed on the pigeon, turning just there above the barn, he hurled the stone, his whole body lunging with its flight.

Quentin staggered, but he kept to his feet. The stone was rising, a slight, hard shimmy in its flight, and it slowed or the pigeon slowed and they were in the same place, in the same moment of stillness after impact, and then the pigeon's wings jerked up and it fell straight down from the sky.

"I got him, Lloyd. By God, I did." Quentin tasted blood on his lip where he had bitten it through, and he moved over the rough ground to where the pigeon had fallen. It was in the matted grass, its beak impaled in mud, and he nudged its body with his foot, and it burbled one last sound and fluttered still.

"I got him," he said again as Lloyd came up.

But he had forgotten the look on Lloyd's face, that look he had seen before of queasiness in the face of death, of killing, that shaking distress that had made Lloyd give up his beef cattle and had surfaced in him for years like the image of some rotting softness at the core of him. Lloyd was silent, twisting his hand on his dog's collar.

Quentin picked up the stone beyond the pigeon and rubbed it in his hand. He bit at the blood on his lip. "Leave it be, Gopher," he said, and the dog stopped sniffing and pawing the pigeon and looked at him. Quentin stared up at the field barn and straightened his cap.

"Those pigeons are settled," he said. "Come on, boy." He turned back to cross the road, and Gopher hobbled up to him.

In the night there was the last of the summer's killer storms. The wind blew out the windows in Quentin's kitchen and scattered Ez Raffin's field barn all across the road and by Monday half of the pigeons were living in the rafters of Quentin's machine shed and the rest had moved to the chimney by his bedroom. Quentin heard them while he slept. He dreamed of them flying toward him in a line that stretched on forever.

When his cousin came on Wednesday, Quentin was standing in the driveway pulling ticks off Gopher.

"You for sure better get rid of them now," his cousin said, watching the pigeons swirl around his chimney.

Quentin shrugged, his gaze lifted to the scatter of boards where the field barn had been. He was finished with it. He'd made up his mind. He knew he was done battling pigeons.

The Killing

When he came home from Vietnam, Montgomery Vonns landed at O'Hare among protesters spitting their banner slogans and jostling him. He did not fly anymore. He took cover in the men's room of Union Station until his train boarded and left to the west and north, hurtling along the river. When he could not stand the incessant ringing in his head, he got up and walked the length of the car. He pulled the door open. In a noise of escaping air and churning metal, he stepped into the freezing cold where the flange of one car butted the next. The car door sucked itself shut. Montgomery lurched against the outside half-door, leaned on it, his head and shoulders sticking into open, rushing space.

Cold burned in streaks across his face, rolled in shock waves through his body. Far ahead of him, the engine raced forward. As hills slid by, flat-topped and congealed with snow, cattle stood on hillsides; tree branches bent groundward in glassy coats of ice.

Montgomery—unmoved—swallowed, inhaled the dryness. When the cold felt too quiet, he drew his head in. The ringing kept on, but he went back inside.

Then he was standing on a platform by the tracks, and though the train had brought him home, he stood in the half-light, the whistle dimming, and he was a stranger, with a stranger's mistrust. He conducted his own reconnaissance. He eyed the start of town with its stone-corniced facades, its flanking white neighborhoods of wooden houses and snow-filled yards that stretched outward toward the country and to the porch beside the county road where his dog Lamb Chop's eyes had blistered gray in death. He realized he would not go home. He did not want the home that waited for him. He wanted, if he could, to disappear.

Open road. Roach clips and three-dollar whiskey. Finally a girl in Santa Fe who laughed easily and made him laugh. She slept in his camouflage jacket and liked his hair curling below his ears and in the black track that skirted his navel. On his knees, Montgomery held the oval swell of her stomach, cradled the rising arc.

At his son's birth, he guided his crowning head, felt the wet contours of his body, but it was his eyes he wanted to see and read, though he could not. He was a soft, purring baby—Jonathan—wondering, wonderless. Seeing him in his mother's arms, Montgomery remembered snow falling through stars while a mare stayed in the softness of the pasture and the moonlight to watch. Remembered the mare feeding earlier, ice in her nostrils but still she sniffed the hay when the sun blued the stable, rays lying down to enter the windows.

As he watched his son grow, Montgomery looked at him warily, watching for the killing gene, that ease of slitting away life that had won him medals in Vietnam. Even when his son was in his crib, he whispered to him from his own darkness. *You take a life like this: a pressure, a swift movement of the hand. Cut. Life leaving. Emptying. And if you feel a coolness then, a watching stillness, you have it. The family gene.*

He had found it in himself at twelve, knew it at eighteen when he watched his buddies grit their teeth in order to bayonet grain-sack dummies, their bodies hurled forward on the order *"Kill!"* Invariably they laughed afterward. They made jokes about gooks. They swaggered and bragged. But piercing the sack, Montgomery felt instead a deadly calm, a familiar sensation of something known.

He waited to discover the same instinct in his son. When Jonathan was twelve, Montgomery in his thoughts could no longer separate Jonathan from himself, from the boy he had been at the same age. In daydreams and nightmares he became Jonathan, and Jonathan him, Monty, feeling the earth of his boyhood shaking under his back from something going by on the road.

Not that small quiver beneath his spine that was like the light touch of seed pods on the field weeds that grazed his legs when he ran to the creek, not that giant movement either, that cradle-like rocking of the whole ditch when a truck passed by, but something in between. Monty raised himself on his elbows and peered over the edge of the ditch. He could see the hubcaps of a car spinning past him in the sun, and he nodded his head and leaned back into the ditch. It was a Ford car all right. An old Galaxy 500. He'd known it from the sound.

Monty pulled his cap down over his forehead and stretched his legs to span the ditch. Sometimes it was five minutes between cars, and he heard other sounds, the creek running if the wind was right, and his sister Rhonda in the house sassing their mother, and maybe the shop sounds, too, his father starting the power tools or pounding out metal.

"Monty, you out there?" The screen door banged shut after Rhonda called him, and he sank down under his hat into the ditch. "We're going in ten minutes. You could get your dirty feet clean."

Clean your own feet, he thought, but he stayed quiet and invisible in the ditch until Lamb Chop came sniffing and barreling over the top of it and swarmed all over him. They were rolling in the dirt. He had his arm around Lamb Chop's neck and Lamb Chop was licking his chin.

"Look at you, you mud hen. You dirt hen." Rhonda loomed over the ditch. "You think Aunt Grace'll let you in her house?"

"Clean your own feet. That goop on your toenails." Monty shook Lamb Chop off and then rolled out of the ditch. He stood up. Maybe ten seconds he stood there, that was all, and when he thought about it later, he knew if Rhonda could mind her own business what happened next never would have. Or even with her meddling, even with her looking for him and waking up Lamb Chop to find him, if he'd just stayed there in the ditch longer. If he'd stretched himself back out again with his head resting on Lamb Chop's belly while it went up and down, the pheasant would have barked by the fence and flown away and Lamb Chop would have trembled, listening, but never really budged. It was her fault and the lady in the Thunderbird ripping down the center line like there was no tomorrow and making it so, in one way anyway, there wasn't. He was blubbering over it all the way to his uncle's place, sitting in the back seat with his face on the window glass, steaming it over.

"Hush up, Monty," his father said, and every time he said it Monty saw it again—the whole thing over, the car coming out of nowhere and Lamb Chop keening on the pheasant and lunging into the road and then stopping like he'd set a brake on, but not in time. Twenty feet up the road where the car had tossed him, Lamp Chop pulled with his front legs to drag himself toward the shoulder, but only one stride, a half a stride before he crumpled onto the pavement and stayed there twitching. Monty had run.

"Pa, Pa," he shouted, and Rhonda was hollering, too, and there were three cars stopped in the road when his father came out on the porch carrying his shotgun. Monty thought the woman was in for it, or her car tires, but it was Lamb Chop his father was after.

He took even aim with the shotgun and Monty rushed him then. "No," he yelled, but his father had pushed him and he was sprawled in the dirt when the gun went off and Lamb Chop reared once in the air and then went still.

Now they were heading for Monty's uncle's place the way they'd planned to do all along. "Want a Kleenex?" Rhonda pushed one at his elbow, and Monty knocked her hand away and rubbed his arm across his nose. They were almost there and he tried holding his breath to shut off the sobs.

"You can get out," his father said. He'd stopped the car in the road before they got to the driveway and he had the door open. "Go wash your face in the creek. Ten minutes, Monty, you be at the barn."

"He'll hurry, Dennis. I guess you can hurry, Monty," his mother said without looking at him, the words floating toward him out of her soft daze, and he pushed against the seat, getting out, and hit running to cross the road.

When he came up behind his uncle's house from the creek, he had his hair wet and slicked back and the salt taste was gone from the corner of his mouth. He could see the men standing by the barn and hear the women laughing on the back porch. "They started doing the chickens yet?" he asked Priscilla, who was his cousin and nine and the youngest cousin he had when there weren't any Martins around. She was on the tire swing eating blackberries.

"Not yet. You been crying, Monty?" She smudged her hands on her shirt. "Aaron's out front if you want him."

"Give me those." He reached in her dish and smeared blackberries by his mouth and under his eyes for war paint and chased her in a big arc past the barn so his father would see him, and on out into the front field which was hayed and full of kids playing ball who were his cousins and his cousins' cousins and their cousins.

"Monty, you pitch," Aaron called, and Monty rubbed the last of the blackberries on his jeans and shook his head.

"My pa wants me." He picked up the ball, which had dribbled up to his feet, and he tossed it back and started for the barn. He was slow walking. He could see his father leaning on the fence by the corner of the barn with tobacco in his jaw. The rest of the men were there, too, his Uncle Rollie and his cousin Troy, his Uncle Henry and Grady Stone with his son-in-law, Roger Stettle. Lawrence Lugar was next to the quarter barrel and so were Lloyd Thomas and Tarr Hansen and

Ez and Charlie Raffin and Bill Toombs and John Mettlie, who'd come back from Vietnam and was marrying Rennie Toombs all the boys were in love with.

"Rollie, you got a paper wasp nest under that rafter," Lawrence Lugar said. He tugged Monty's hair. "Looks like you tangled with a nest of blackberries, Monty. You come eat some at our house. Pauline put turkey manure on the berry patch and they got too big for the jar."

"Answer him, Monty," Dennis Vonns said and when Monty did, his father looked at him with his still eyes. "Montgomery had himself a tragedy today. His dog got killed."

Lloyd Thomas pulled the toothpick out of his mouth. "The one from the litter with mine?"

Monty nodded and listened to his father. "Some woman with a T-bird went right into him. I had to shoot the poor bastard."

"We got us some pups," Tarr Hansen said. "Part spaniel. You want one, Monty, you talk to Knobby."

"No," Monty said, and that was all he said, looking at his father and his locked-in gray eyes and knowing, because his Uncle Rollie had told him that, as a boy, his father had tied a bucking mare to a fence and left the autumn burrs on her face until her eyes mattered shut.

Lawrence blew his nose into a big red handkerchief. "Looks like the women got the food ready. We can get our strength up for those chickens."

It wasn't until Monty had his plate filled up and was sitting next to a tree that he knew he wasn't hungry. "I got you the end piece of the ham," Rhonda said, stopping in front of him.

"Get lost," he said. He watched Rhonda sit down on the grass next to Brianne Hansen, who was eating a bun with one hand and holding Jerry Raffin's hand with the other. Brianne's sisters were sitting on the grass, too, Branch and Brenda and Bronwyn, though not Knobby, who was the youngest Hansen and actually Joyce but got called Knobby for "No-B" since she hadn't been Brandon. She was dangling her feet out of a tree so they were practically inside Jerry's collar.

"You feel all right, Monty?" Aaron's little sister was looking at him. "You could go on a leaf like those green caterpillars without showing."

"He does look green. You're right, Tanya," Sally Raffin said, and Monty stuck his fork in his Jell-O and turned it over. He looked over at Diane Stone feeding her baby, Cherry Jane Stettle, with a deviled egg that had got spread all over her face.

"Leave him be, Tanya," Rhonda said.

"Well he does look green," Tanya said, and Aaron's oldest sisters, Maria, who was learning to be a nurse, and Lara, who was training to be a bank teller, said he did, too, and Monty figured out the whole place was full of somebody's sisters. For boys, it was only Jerry Raffin and Peter Stone who hung around the men mostly and Teddy Raffin, who was seven and didn't count, and Aaron and him and Steve Lugar, who'd been on a camping trip and was asleep in the Lugars' truck.

"Buzz off, Tanya," Monty said. He felt hot, all of a sudden, and funny in the stomach and, sticking his plate down by his glass, he got up in a hurry and took off running for the house.

He was in the bathroom a long time. Then he heard his father outside the door. "You in there, Monty? Come on out."

"I threw up, Pa," he said.

"It's time for the chickens," Dennis Vonns said. Monty splashed water on his face and then flushed the toilet. He opened the door. The hall outside the door was dark. It smelled of old wood. Monty thought of his father in the Grayhill School picture: second from the end in the second row, wearing suspenders and rolled-cuff pants. Clean. Almost neat. Sturdy shoes and brushed hair and his body tightly banded with his striped T-shirt.

"Was it your mother's bars? You eat those?" Dennis Vonns said and Monty thought he was smiling at his joke, though he couldn't really see.

There were women in the kitchen scraping dishes when they went through, and Monty was headed toward the door when his father stopped him with a hand on his collar. "Grace, you got something for his stomach? I guess he ate some of Dora's bars."

"I thought they were yours, Dennis," Pauline Lugar said, and all the women laughed, except Monty's mother, who was looking out the window as if she'd never heard a thing. His Aunt Grace rummaged in the cabinet for some Pepto-Bismol and then poured it out pink.

"There you go, Monty," she said, and she asked the women if they'd gotten their hands on Diane and Roger's new baby, and Linda Raffin said as long as it wasn't her niece showing up with a baby.

Her mother, Belle Toombs, shushed her. "Dennis, are they ready with the chickens?" she asked and when he nodded on his way to the door, Pauline said they'd be out in two minutes and to have Rollie wait long enough so Belle could do the first one.

Outside the men had the gate open to the chicken yard, and Grady Stone told Peter and Jerry they could do the catching.

"These are fat birds," Lawrence Lugar said. "Look at that drumstick. Rollie, how many you say we lost?"

"Five. Maybe six. Nothing out of two hundred. Priscilla, is the water boiled? Where'd Priscilla get to? Aaron, you and Monty go look in the shed and see if Tina's got the water ready."

When they came back and said that she did, everyone was in front of the chicken yard except Ez Raffin, who wasn't back from milking yet, and Lloyd and Ella Thomas, who were leaving in Lloyd's truck. The women were there with their aprons on and Grady Stone had the piece of stump for chopping ready with the nails in to hold the chicken's necks.

"I don't need that. You can move that away from the gate," Belle Toombs said. "You want me to kill the first one I'll cut its head off like I always do." She had her sleeves rolled up and her butcher knife ready, and Monty saw her hair was purpler this time from the beauty shop. "Grady, where's your dad? You giving us old folks the honors, he better get out here too."

"Come on, Pa," Grady Stone said and Graydon Stone Sr., who was really just Pa Stone ever since Grady took the Jr. off his name, gave Victoria Stone the box of leftover poppies from Decoration Day he'd been trying to peddle ever since he arrived. He stepped out next to Belle Toombs.

"It's killing—just like in the war, Pa," Grady said, and everybody laughed, but easy and friendly like, because everybody put up with it that all Pa Stone ever talked about was being in the war. The *Great* War.

"You want me to do what, Belle?" he said. He was stooped over and he had a poppy on his hat and one on his shirt next to his Legion pin, and Monty thought that with his bowed legs he looked older than anybody he'd ever seen.

"Get us a chicken, Jerry," Rollie Vonns said and Jerry Raffin went into the chicken coop and came out a second later carrying a chicken by its legs that was squawking bloody murder and trying to reach around and peck him.

"You hold him, Graydon," Belle said. "Hold him tight now."

"If I can get him." Pa Stone was hobbling around Jerry trying to catch the chicken's legs. Then he grabbed on. "Let him go, Jerry. First thing I held tight maybe in twenty years."

He had the chicken by the legs, one leg and a wing in each hand, and Belle started sawing with her knife. "Keep a hold of him, Graydon!" she said, but the chicken had a wing free and then it spurted loose and was jerking crazily around the yard with its head flapping from its neck.

"What a mess," Belle said, and everybody was laughing and pushing to get out of the way while the chicken kept running in circles and the blood squirted out of its neck. It dropped finally and sputtered still and Rollie Vonns reached down with his pocketknife and cut through the bit of skin that was holding the head on.

"Get it dunked, Tina," he said, "and you kids can take the feathers off."

It was started then. Monty moved out of the way of Pa Stone who was walking by him rubbing his wrist. They all had their parts, he knew, after Belle Toombs the men to do the killing, the kids to pluck, and the women to clean. He looked up at the sky, past the fir tree at the end of the chicken coop that had needles hanging from it like so much wet laundry, a fir tree like the one he'd climbed before his father cut it down when he logged out the woods. It had hung suspended over the creek, each hair-gnarled root straining to pull free.

Monty was seeing spots between the branches that were maybe from looking at the sun and maybe from the blood spots the chicken had left staining the dust. There had been blood from Lamb Chop, too, a little pool of blood that trickled out of the corner of his mouth.

"You coming?" Aaron asked.

Monty went with him and looked in the shed where Tina was dipping the chicken down into the first kettle by its legs.

"We need the garbage cans," Aaron said.

When they had hauled them up from the woodshed, the girls had the chicken stripped down to its skin. "I can't get the pinfeathers," Knobby said, rubbing at her nose with the back of her hand, and Aaron took his pliers out of his back pocket and picked the chicken up.

"You're getting grease on it with those. Yuk," Sally Raffin told him, and Aaron kept pulling the pinfeathers out anyway and then smudged the stains lighter with his fingers.

"Nobody'll know," he said.

There was another chicken on the way now, and another and another. Grady Stone was doing the first batch, dragging the chickens across the stump so their necks stretched out caught between the nails and then swinging down with his hatchet to chop the heads off. Jerry and Peter were going in and out of the chicken coop like it had a revolving door.

"It's not fair," Priscilla said. "We get the worst part. All these hot, squishy feathers. Knobby, how come all your sisters are cleaning this year?"

"They think they're grown up." Knobby waited a second with her hand up and then sneezed. "They can have it. I sure wouldn't want to reach inside of a chicken."

Monty had the feathers off three chickens and he picked up the two he'd laid on a newspaper and carried all three over to the tables where the women were doing the cleaning.

"Here, Ma," he said. He put the chickens down on the table in front of her and she looked at him the way she always did, like she'd just woken up from a nap. He stayed watching her arrange the chickens. She pressed down on the legs of all three while she cut off their claws.

His Aunt Grace was wrapping a butchered chicken. "Monty, tell Tina she's keeping them in too long. That last one I got was half boiled."

"Go on, Monty," his mother said. "Your pa'll say you're goldbricking."

When he got done talking to Tina, there were two more chickens on his pile. He started rubbing feathers.

"Give me your pliers, Aaron," he said. He could see the men and hear them joking over by the chicken yard. It was Lawrence's turn, and a yell and whistle went up every time he stunned a chicken with the tire iron and stuck his knife in its neck to bleed it, which was his way of killing a chicken.

"You trying to set a record for fast, Lawrence? I'll show you fast," Charlie Raffin said.

Tarr Hansen was sipping his beer. "We know how fast you are. That why Tess took her vacation without you?"

Lawrence was laughing, and he stuck the knife in the last chicken and let it run. "OK. Let's see your fast," he said. He picked his chicken up and dumped it on the pile he'd made, and Charlie Raffin took hold of the chicken Peter Stone was carrying out of the coop and snapped his wrist hard so the chicken swung up and over his hand and broke its neck.

"There," Charlie said laying the chicken down on the ground. "Get me another one."

"You get those wrists playing with the fire hose?" Grady Stone asked.

Monty craned a little to watch Charlie, but he kept glancing back, too, to pull more pinfeathers until he had his chicken clean. "You hot, Aaron?" he said, taking his shirt off and hanging it on the fence. His stomach was still a little funny and he didn't know when it was he was going to eat any chicken again. He looked at Knobby and Priscilla with their red faces and sweaty hair, and then over at the women's tables, where enormous stacks of butchered chickens were piling up, each chicken sealed up in freezer wrap. He could hear the knives whacking against the tables and now and again he got a whiff of the chicken innards the women pulled out.

"If you're getting lemonade, bring us all some," Aaron said to Rhonda, who was walking across the yard carrying a chicken. When she came back with a tray of glasses, Monty looked at them and then went over to the pump and got a drink of water.

"I didn't poison yours. Maybe I should have," Rhonda said, and he figured she was over feeling guilty now and he didn't have to listen any more to her trying to be nice.

It was five chickens later when his fingers were stiff and his thumb all bloody, that his father came up to him. "You ready?" Dennis Vonns said. Monty looked at him.

"I got the killing next. I need you to help."

"I got more feathers to do."

"Let Rhonda do it. Come on." His father was looking at him with a steady eye and there was something in his look that made Monty think of Lamb Chop and how he was when he brought the ducks back in hunting season.

"It's hot, Pa," he said. He pushed his cap back on his head and rubbed the sweat away, but then he followed his father over to the chicken coop.

"How you want to do it, Dennis?" Ez Raffin said. "You got a lazy way maybe with your boy helping?"

"Maybe," Dennis Vonns said. "Maybe not. Monty, you hold while I cut their heads off. And you hold good. I don't want you to Pa Stone me."

Monty was looking off toward the pasture where his uncle's heifers were butting each other and then leaping up the hill, their tails swinging like lariats, and he was seeing spots again, with the sunshine coming in low into his eyes.

"You just hold good," his father said.

And it wasn't then like anything Monty had ever known. He'd shot birds. He'd seen them fall out of the sky and he'd aimed at squirrels in the woods and tried for deer. But this was different. Peter was pushing the chicken at him and Monty was struggling with his fingers to catch the wings against its legs, and the whole weight of it was lunging and pulling away from him.

"Just keep holding, Monty," his father said and Monty saw the knife ready in his hands, and what he meant to do was look past it all, to stare hard into the field where the hay was spotted around like giant rolls of shredded wheat, to see just that, but the chicken was screaming and Monty looked at it instead and his father cutting, cool, impassive, and he felt the chicken legs stretched out from his arms and the chicken yanking at the end of them, jerking heavily like a car with its clutch popped.

"He's stopped now. You can let him go," his father said, and Monty did and the men were quiet around him. He looked at the clot of blood smeared across his jeans leg.

"How many more we got, Grady?" Dennis Vonns said, and it was all like that, the rest of it, matter-of-fact, with more chickens coming, more chicken heads landing in the pile by the gate, and the men talking and Monty holding chickens until he had the feel of it, the life erupting out of them.

"What're you doing with that dog, Dennis?" Tarr Hansen said and Dennis Vonns told him, cutting his way through a chicken's neck. "I hung him in the shed away from the animals. Monty'll bury him in the morning."

"You could freeze him, Dennis. You hear about the fellow that was house-sitting and dog-sitting and the dog got killed and the fellow saved him for the owner all laid out in the freezer?"

"I could of done that to my cow. My best cow died last winter and maybe if I'd have froze her, someday I could of thawed her out at the vet's so he could fix her up."

"My pa's cat is what we should of done it to. That cat was the damnedest thing. It was black and the only thing it would eat was food like orange ice cream and cantaloupe. It was like a Halloween cat, and Pa always thought he could make some money off of it, but it died."

They were talking. There were all the stories they thought of and the ones they wouldn't think of about the sons that weren't here— their boys off at war in the jungle. Then with dusk falling, Peter came out and took his hat off the fence post. "There's only one left. Jerry's bringing it," he said and Monty rubbed some dirt on the blood on his stomach and looked at his father, and the heat of the air seemed to rise right up inside him and fling him upward, the way the bullet had hurled Lamb Chop. Then it dropped him back to earth and it was gone. The heat was just gone.

"I'll kill it, Pa," he said, looking at him steadily, at the stone-hard fact of him, at the man known by the trails he left: stripped carcasses, trees lying down a hillside like a scatter of pickup sticks.

"He can use the stump," Dennis Vonns said. He leaned past Monty and took the screeching chicken from Jerry and stretched its neck out through the nails and it went still, and Monty brought the hatchet down.

It was afterward that he saw the lights in the sky. It was while the women were butchering the last of the chickens in the light from the porch and the men had turned the water on to hose down the chicken yard and the kids were yelling and running in the spray and, in the driveway, people were starting their good-byes, Cherry Jane Stettle crying in her grandmother Victoria's arms while her parents left for the drive-in. It was only then that Monty saw the sky turn from dark blue to green.

He was leaning on the chicken coop turning the hatchet in his hand and watching Jerry Raffin charge up and down the hay field on Tina's colt while she hollered at him, and he thought first that the light flickering was just something flashing off and on inside of him from the heat. Then he looked up and he saw it was the sky, the whole of it to the north lit up like fireworks igniting and bands of green the color of an Asian jungle—bands of streaking green like huge, curving fluorescent tubes. It was only then that he saw the lights—only then, after he'd killed the last chicken. But standing there, his eyes moving on the sky, Monty saw it as a sign fully manifest.

"I'll be in the car, Pa," he said, laying the hatchet on the log and squaring his hat around. Monty stood up straight and crossed the yard, though in his nightmare in the dry heat of Santa Fe, it is Jonathan who gets in the car and slams the door.

ACKNOWLEDGMENTS

Versions of these stories and novella have appeared in *Puerto del Sol* ("In the Land of the Dinosaur"), *Great River Review* ("The Home of the Wet T-Shirt Contest"), *Wisconsin Academy Review* ("At Flood Tide"), the *Rockford Review* ("Anthony Martin Is Dead"), *American Fiction* ("A Carnival of Animals"), *Passages North* ("Hubbub, Indigo, Castle of Rain" as "What Is a Hubbub and Spell Indigo"), *Snake Nation Review* ("Turkey Run"), and *Sands* ("Violin Song" and "A Marriage in the Life of Faith Davenport"), the *Threepenny Review* ("The Battle"), and the *Greensboro Review* ("The Killing").